VIRGINIA IRONSIDE has wo
on a number of publicatic
Daily Mail and *Woman* – ⸱ ⸱⸱⸱⸱⸱y ⸱⸱⸱
editor of *The Sunday Mirror*'s problem page.
Poltergeist of Burlap Hall is her fourth title
about the pupils and staff of a gothic boarding
school; the others are *Vampire Master*, *Spaceboy at Burlap Hall* and *Phantom of Burlap
Hall*. She has also written two stories for
younger readers, *Roseanne and the Magic
Mirror* and *The Human Zoo* (both published
by Walker Books), and three novels for adults.
Virginia Ironside lives in West London with
her son.

Other books by Virginia Ironside

Phantom of Burlap Hall
Spaceboy at Burlap Hall
Vampire Master

For younger readers

The Human Zoo
Roseanne and the Magic Mirror

THE POLTERGEIST OF BURLAP HALL

VIRGINIA IRONSIDE

WALKER BOOKS
LONDON

First published 1993 by Walker Books Ltd
87 Vauxhall Walk, London SE11 5HJ

Text © 1993 Virginia Ironside
Cover illustration © 1993 Mick Brownfield

This book has been typeset in Sabon.

Printed in England by
Clay Ltd, St Ives plc

British Library Cataloguing in Publication Data
A catalogue record for this book
is available from the British Library.

ISBN 0-7445-2444-X

For
Selina Hastings

CHAPTER ONE

LANCHESTER LARRY FOUND MURDERED! The headline from the *Lanchester Gazette* screamed out at Mr Fox among the muddle of letters, unpaid bills and empty half-bottles of whisky. The news didn't put the headmaster of Burlap Hall in any better mood. He sighed and then he leant forward. He rested one elbow on a card which read: "Just to inform you that my son, Alfred, has had an accident and will not be returning to school. That is the reason we have not paid our term's fees in advance." The other elbow rested on a bill on which was printed in red: "Final Notice! Non-payment of this bill will result in your electricity being cut off!" He placed his head in his hands and groaned. Far away, the wail of an ambulance screamed into the open country, suitably reflecting his mood.

"Oh, pessimissimus," he wailed to himself. "Oh, pessimissimissi–issi–issi–issimus!"

The day before the beginning of term was the one that Mr Fox dreaded even more than his pupils, who were at this very moment descending from all parts of the country, by boat, plane, train and car, on the huge old gothic pile in the middle of Lanchestershire. Why was it that he never got his act together early enough? Why was it always the same? He fumbled around for his diary, found the date of the beginning of the following term and, counting back a fortnight, wrote a note to himself: "Get organized for next term *now*!"

He shut it again. But that wouldn't solve the troubles he was having with *this* term. This, the summer term, was the one when there was a Parents' Day, when all the parents of pupils already at the school and parents of pupils wishing to come to the school (and God knows there were few enough of them) assembled in a variety of silly hats and posh suits and demanded to discuss their children's work with the teachers and watch dancing displays and swimming tournaments and who knows what. And should the Parents' Day be on June 14th? Or June 15th? And did it matter one jot? No, it made not a blind bit of difference – but when you don't want it to be either day it's amazing how difficult it is, thought Mr Fox, to make up your mind.

There was a soft knock on his door. Relaxing slightly in the hopes that it might be a nice cup of tea brought by Mr Crumbly, the caretaker, Mr Fox swept the empty whisky bottles (which he'd found while turning out an old filing cabinet) into the wastepaper basket and covered them with a report from the Department of Education. Then he shuffled papers around, making a rustling noise so that the person outside would think he was busy, and said, in a "Don't-interrupt-me-I'm-working-really-hard" kind of voice: "Yes?"

It wasn't a cup of tea. It was Mr Fritz, the deputy headmaster and science teacher, who had arrived early this term to help Mr Fox with the administration problems.

He wore a hairy, tweed suit that made him look like a hedgehog, he had a small goatee beard and on his nose was balanced a pair of spectacles held together with sticking plaster. He looked worried.

"Bad news, I'm afraid," he said.

Mr Fox stared at him glumly and raised his eyebrows. At least, he thought as he raised them, he still *had* his eyebrows. Most of the hair on his head had fallen out, except for a few long strands that he combed carefully over his bald patch; but his eyebrows – so far – were intact.

"It's Mr Crumbly," said Mr Fritz.

Suddenly Mr Fox remembered the wail of the ambulance.

"Are we saying," he said, fearfully, "that Mr Crumbly has finally crumbled?"

"We are," said Mr Fritz. "Which means that we are lacking one caretaker."

"Is he..." There was a faint look of hope in Mr Fox's eyes.

"Oh, no," said Mr Fritz. "At least, not yet. Almost. There is, of course, always a chance... But a severe heart attack is never very promising." They looked at each other and both knew what the other was thinking. Then they pretended to look very serious and downcast. Mr Crumbly had been the caretaker at Burlap Hall for yonks. Or even, indeed, pre-yonks, if there were such a time. He seemed to come with the building. And he certainly was in a similar state of repair. It took him about six weeks to replace a pane of glass, three weeks to fix a light bulb, a couple of days to change a plug, and as for mowing the lawn, it seemed to Mr Fox that he did it only once a year.

"Let's look on the bright side," said Mr Fritz. "We could get a temporary replacement who might be full of energy and pizazz."

"Perwhat?" said Mr Fox, wrinkling his brow.

"Pizazz," said Mr Fritz. "Oomph. Drive. Beans. Go."

"He could certainly weed the drive," said

Mr Fox, puzzled. "And getting him to plant beans is a good idea. Save on vegetables. But I don't like the idea of him going. The idea is for him to stay, surely."

Mr Fritz sighed. "You were going down to Lanchester this afternoon," he said. "Why don't you pop into the Job Centre and see if they've got anyone in need of a temporary caretaking job?"

"Good idea, Fritz," said Mr Fox, jumping up at the prospect of getting away. "And in the meantime, perhaps you could..." He glanced at the pile of bills and papers on his desk.

"Certainly," said Mr Fritz, moving round to Mr Fox's chair and starting to sort out the papers. "Ah, Parents' Day. When is it? June fourteenth?"

"Whenever you like," said Mr Fox wearily. "You decide. And make sure the invitations go out. And if you could organize payment..."

"Oh, look – poor old Lanchester Larry!" said Mr Fritz, spotting the headline in the paper.

Mr Fox glanced down and read through the story swiftly. "Well, that'll teach him to get a job and not spend his time sleeping in bus shelters in Lanchester!" he snapped rather unsympathetically.

"Bit late to teach him, isn't it?" said Mr Fritz. "Hmm. They're looking for a man with a dog... And there's a memorial service at St

Agnes. A sad story…"

But Mr Fox was already hurrying down the stairs into his car.

There was nothing like stepping out into the bright, crisp sunshine to put a spring in your step and a gleam in your eye, thought Mr Fox as he bowled along towards Lanchester. A new caretaker! Mr Fritz was right. There was so much unemployment these days, too, that a professional carpenter desperate for a roof over his head and a few school dinners could probably be snapped up for a couple of pounds a week. He could build cupboards, fix the banisters, French polish the tables. Assuming Mr Crumbly was away for long enough, Mr Fox would have him slaving away for weeks for peanuts. And if the old man recovered too quickly, Mr Fox could always insist he convalesced…

At the Job Centre, a run-down building squashed between Our Price and W H Smith, Mr Fox pushed through what seemed to him like hordes of unemployed louts and sat down in front of a wispy-looking woman with a sour expression on her face.

"Name?" she said, not looking up. "Age?" Mr Fox gave both, but so reluctantly that she barked, "Are you interested or not? Or are you just a time-waster?"

"I am certainly not a time-waster!"

"Good. GCSEs? If any?"

Mr Fox exploded. "If any?" he snorted. "Why, I am at Burlap Hall, and I don't see what my GCSEs – or O levels as they were in my day – have got to do with it."

"Still at school?" she said, staring at the form she was filling in. "And O levels? Oh, well, Burlap Hall's such an old-fashioned heap I shouldn't be surprised if they've never heard of the new Curriculum. But if you're still at school there's no point looking for a job. Come back when you've left. Next please!"

"MADAM!" said Mr Fox, rising to his feet and giving her one of his famous looks. His brows bristled like prickles on a porcupine, his cheeks went a funny purple colour, his neck bulged like an aggressive toad and his ears glowed like a pair of light-up bow ties.

"MADAM!" he repeated, thrusting his face into hers. "I am not looking for a job! I am the headmaster of Burlap Hall, that old-fashioned heap as you call it, and I will have you know that if it weren't for people like me, trying to give jobs to decent citizens, there wouldn't be people like you behind a desk, looking for people to give jobs to, because there wouldn't be any. Then *you* would be coming here for a job, except there wouldn't be a here to come to because there would be no people like me to...!"

The woman finally looked up and, going

bright red, burbled her apologies. "I didn't realize you were looking to *employ* someone," she said. "I'm ever so sorry." She pulled a new form from a drawer. "Now, let me take the details."

When the issue was finally sorted out, Mr Fox was faced with two alternatives: an ex-Buddhist monk who, unfortunately, had a prison record, one leg, no references, but a double first in theology; and a Mr Ron Grunt, odd-jobman and casual labourer. He sounded the best bet, particularly as he was, for some reason, very anxious to move out of his flat.

Mr Fox decided to pay him a visit. There was no time like the present – and if he could return to the school with the matter settled, so much the better. He made a quick detour to his favourite wine merchant, Booze 'n' Binends, to pick up a couple of cases of whisky, and then made his way to Ron Grunt's address.

Ron Grunt lived above a used-metal scrap dealer's yard. The door was sprayed with pictures of skulls. There was no bell, and Mr Fox hesitated before knocking. After about five minutes a window was lifted upstairs and a pasty-faced, unshaven individual stared down. He appeared to be wearing a string vest.

"'Oo is it?" he yelled angrily.

"My name's Mr Fox, from Burlap Hall," said the headmaster nervously. "I've come about a job – I mean about a job I'd like to offer you. Temporary caretaker."

"Yer wha…?" said the man, screwing up his eyes as he peered down.

"Is this the right house?" asked Mr Fox, looking again at the door. "I'm looking for a Mr Grunt."

The man upstairs exploded with laughter. "Grunt. That's me. Give me a couple of minutes."

There was a loud clanking and chinking noise as Ron Grunt unlatched a door that seemed as closely barred as Fort Knox. He was a hideous-looking individual, about five foot tall and approximately the same width, grimy muscle bursting out of the torn, oil-stained T-shirt that he had hurriedly put on. He wore no shoes and his toenails were long and curved, like an animal's. His breath reeked of beer.

"Good heavens, your house is as secure as a prison!" said Mr Fox, shaking Ron Grunt by the hand.

"Prison?" said Ron angrily. "I've never been to prison and I don't intend to in the near future, either."

Mr Fox thought he was most peculiar. He didn't look at all suitable for a caretaker. He had a huge potbelly and on his arms were tattoos of naked ladies, snakes and lions.

"If you came to us, I would have to insist that you wore, er … to cover up, er … as it's a school."

Ron Grunt laughed cheerfully. "OK, Mr Fox," he said. "I'm game. I expect there's a lot of work to do up there, ain't there? Bet those godfers do a lot of damage, eh? And after all, it must be a big arse and all that."

"Godfers?" said Mr Fox in a baffled way. "And as for big arse," he added, rather shocked. "*Do* you mind!"

"Godfers – kids. Rhyming slang. God forbid, kid. As for arse – big h-arse," said Ron Grunt. "Harse."

"Oh, house," said Mr Fox, relieved.

"That's right. Harse," said Ron Grunt, laughing. "You thought I meant a Khyber, didn't you – Khyber Pass, arse. We'll make a cockney of you yet. I'll teach you words you never knew you didn't know. I like you, Mr Fox. The moment I set eyes on you I said to myself: That is a proper gentleman."

Mr Fox blushed deep red and drew himself up. He had been wrong about Ron Grunt, he decided. This man might look like an escaped convict, but he had judgement. Anyone who recognized him as a proper gentleman must have rare qualities. He made an instant decision. He held out his hand and Ron took it. They shook.

"Well," said Ron Grunt. "I'll come back to the school with you. I want to get away as soon as possible."

"Are you ready?" asked Mr Fox, surprised.

"I can always give you a lift. You're right. No time like the present."

"Prison?" said Ron Grunt, suspiciously. "You didn't say prison?"

"No, 'present'. Though perhaps you need an hour or two to tidy up?"

Ron Grunt seemed to think this incredibly funny, but he just said, "I'll be a couple of ticks. You wait here."

He soon appeared with a small holdall, a large black plastic bin-bag tied tight at the neck and a four-pack of lager.

Mr Fox looked rather disapproving.

"We don't really like our staff to drink. At least not on duty," he said.

"Don't worry," said Ron Grunt. "I'll 'ave polished them off by the time we get to the school." He cracked open the first can and started pouring it down his throat. "Right, Mr Fox. Ready to go!" With his free hand he locked the front door with a huge key, and they set off for Mr Fox's car.

"So what kind of lah-di-dah've you got? A Rolls? A BMW?"

"Lah-di-dah?" said Mr Fox, puzzled. "Do you mean car? I've got a Morris Minor."

"That's what I like to hear," said Ron Grunt, taking Mr Fox rather too familiarly by the arm. "Easy to break into, mind, but then who'd want to break into a Morris Minor, I always say!" He roared with laughter. "Why buy a car alarm when you could buy a Morris Minor instead?"

"Certainly no one has ever tried to break into my car," said Mr Fox, with furrowed brow, as he scanned the street nervously for his old banger.

"That's the spirit," said Ron Grunt. "You and I are going to get on fine!" As they passed a low wall, Ron Grunt hurled his bin-bag over it.

Mr Fox looked at him in surprise.

"Just rubbish," said Ron Grunt casually.

Though the headmaster thought it was rather strange, he thought no more of it. And it was only as they reached the car and he fumbled around for the keys that he noticed an enormous, black dog growling at his ankles.

"There seems to be a dog here," he said. "It's followed us from the scrapyard!"

"Oh, yeah, Tyson. A big baby," replied Ron, calling him over. "Didn't they tell you abart the dog at the Job Centre?"

"No..." said Mr Fox.

"Oh, he comes with me," said Ron, smiling amiably.

At this point Mr Fox, who was having second thoughts about his new employee, thought he saw a let-out.

"Oh, I'm ever so sorry," he said, sighing with relief. "But I'm afraid we can't allow dogs at Burlap Hall. It would be far too dangerous with the pupils. I mean, er, the godfers. So sorry to put you to this trouble."

Ron Grunt looked suddenly menacing. "You going back on our gentleman's agreement?" he said threateningly. "I don't like a man who goes back on an agreement. Tell you what," he said, as he mysteriously opened the locked passenger door and let his gigantic dog into the back seat, "I'll keep him locked up all the time. If anyone spots him, he's called Lucy, OK? And if there's any trouble, you can chuck me out after three months with only a week's notice. Fair enough?"

Since the dog was already in the car there was no way Mr Fox could, as he had hoped, leap in and just leave Ron and his dog standing. Reluctantly he got into the driving seat, nodding his head nervously. Ron got in beside him and then turned to give his dog a pat. As he did so, he spotted the case of whisky that Mr Fox had put on the back seat.

"One rule for the masters and another for the servants, eh?" he said, rather unpleasantly. He opened the second of his four-pack. "Want some of me pig's?" he asked.

Mr Fox's mind swam. "Pigs?" he said. Dogs, pigs, he couldn't keep up.

"Pig's ear, beer," said Ron, opening a new can which spurted all over Mr Fox's dashboard. "Well, he's a Dobermann pinscher."

"A Dobermann pinscher!" said Mr Fox.

"But they're the fiercest dogs in the world!"

"Oh, he's not all Dobermann. Nah. He's a cross-breed."

"Crossed," said Mr Fox, as he nervously put the key into the ignition and feeling the dog's hot smelly breath on the nape of his neck, "with what?"

"Pit bull," said Ron. "And just a teensy, teensy drop of something else."

"What?" said Mr Fox, not daring to look at the animal growling behind him.

"Rottweiler," said Ron, cheerily. "And now, we'd better get going, if you don't mind, Mr Fox, because Tyson – I mean, Lucy – doesn't like hanging around in cars."

Mr Fox closed his eyes, wishing he were dead. He had a deadly, sinking feeling that Ron Grunt was a big, big mistake. But as a whiff of Tyson's evil breath came his way, he opened his eyes quickly, got into first gear, and drove back to Burlap Hall as fast as he could.

Tom, Miles and Susan and a bunch of other Burlap Hallers who had arrived by train had been waiting an hour on Lanchester Station. It was eight o'clock and starting to get dark. They were usually met by Mr Crumbly, who drove the school bus to meet the train. But so far there was no sign of him.

Trains had come and gone, delivering businessmen, farmers and old ladies returning from day trips. But now even the station master was gathering up his things to go home and the birds had all but packed up their final chattering to return to their nests. The whole station glowed with the deep, hot, evening haze of summer.

"He's always late," said Miles, who'd been at the school longer than any of them.

"Oh, well, the later he is the better," said Susan, a frizzy-haired American girl. "Every minute means the term's shorter."

Tom came over to the pair who were sitting gloomily on their suitcases. He was fourteen years old with long tousled hair, having escaped his mother's entreaties to visit the barber at the end of the holidays. He sat down on a bench nearby and idly picked up an abandoned copy of the *Lanchester Gazette*.

"Still no sign of Mr Crumbly?" said Asquith Minor, wandering up. "Poor old thing. The heat's probably got to him at last. By the way, did you hear about the idiot who said 'No'?"

"No," said Susan, walking into the trap.

Everyone laughed. Susan frowned, cross at being caught out. Then Tom looked up from the paper, saying, "Hey, listen to this! Lanchester Larry's been murdered!"

"What?" Susan and Miles were horrified. "In Lanchester? But there are no murders in Lanchester! Read it out!"

"'An old tramp of no fixed address was

found stabbed to death in a bus shelter in the early hours of this morning. He is believed to have been known as "Lanchester Larry", a harmless vagrant who for the last three years had taken up residence in the Lanchester bus shelter. A colourful local character, always fond of a drink, Lanchester Larry was renowned for his good humour. "We all loved Larry," said Miss Atkins, the postmistress. "He would never harm a fly. He always had a good word for everyone even when he'd had a few." Larry's body was discovered by an off-duty policeman... Police are looking for a man who was walking his dog at the time of the killing to eliminate him from their enquiries. The dog is thought to go by the name of...' blahdi, blahdi blah...

"'This is the first recorded murder since 1643 in the sleepy fifteenth-century town of Lanchester, a peaceful haven...' Had enough?"

"Oh, it must have been horrible. But why should anyone murder Larry?" asked Susan. "He never had any money to steal."

"I remember Larry," said Miles. "Harmless but always drunk."

"I once gave him ten pence," said Tom sadly, remembering the tramp's matted hair, his filthy jeans and mittened hands. "He said it was for a cup of tea. Do you remember his smell?"

Miles held his nose. "Ugh, who wouldn't!" he said.

Simon came up. "Heard about the gory murder?" he said. "By the way, where's old Crumbly?"

It was getting quite dark. Suddenly, after reading about Lanchester Larry's murder, it wasn't such fun hanging around on the deserted platform. Who knew? Perhaps the murderer could be... As the ticket inspector walked by, they found themselves shrinking into the shadows. It could be anyone!

"I'll ring up the school," said Tom. "And find out what's happening."

"Oh, do," said Sheila, coming up with her case. "I'm bored and this place is starting to give me the creeps."

The fact was that, in the drama of everyone arriving and getting themselves sorted out, Mr Crumbly's chauffeuring duties had been forgotten. But Tom's call reminded them and eventually the school bus arrived. Mr Carstairs, the English teacher who also took sports and games, jumped out and shook them all jovially by the hands.

"Hope you had great hols!" he enthused. "Expect you thought we'd forgotten about you. And we had! Everyone else is at the school and I'd only just arrived when I was told to go off and fetch you. Poor old Mr

Crumbly had a heart attack so we were one man short."

Everyone piled into the bus as Mr Carstairs loaded their cases into the back. They were relieved to be on their way at last. As they settled down, Mr Carstairs pointed to the back of the driver's head before shutting the back doors.

"Ron Grunt – our temporary caretaker," he said, "who has only just arrived. May I introduce you?" As Mr Carstairs made his way outside to the front passenger seat, Ron turned, and gave a sinister grin. "Wotcher, kids," he said. "And no messin' abart wiv old Ron 'ere, right?"

Tom, Miles and the rest looked at each other in astonishment. That wasn't how Mr Crumbly used to address them. Until recently, indeed, he called all the boys "sir" and all the girls "miss" and only in the last year had been persuaded to call them "Mister Tom", "Miss Susan" and so on.

"Right, lads?" said Ron, turning round again. "Until I get an answer, we're stickin' right 'ere."

"Right!" everyone mumbled hastily. But Susan said, "Excuse me, but Sheila and I aren't lads."

"Wiv respect," said Ron, in an unpleasant voice, "shut your face, me old darlin'. And in future I'll be keepin' my minces on you, OK?"

He gave Susan a threatening glare.

Mr Carstairs got into the front seat, and Ron Grunt put the bus into gear and drove off.

Asquith Minor made joky cowering gestures, shrinking into his jacket, and Simon explained that "minces" were "eyes", as in mince pies. Meanwhile, Tom nudged Miles and pointed, because coiling from Ron's shirt collar, and about to stretch into his cropped hair, was a tattooed snake. Everyone started to giggle, but the noise was drowned by the roar of the engine as the van rattled into the darkness towards Burlap Hall.

From the very moment Ron had got into Mr Fox's car, things had started to go disastrously wrong. The clutch had started slipping, the steering went wonky, the driving seat suddenly slipped right back just as Mr Fox was overtaking an old lady on a bicycle. And finally, when they arrived at the school, and Ron and his dog got out, all the tyres had simultaneously punctured, in front of Mr Fox's very eyes. He turned to Ron, warily. He had never known such a thing.

But Ron appeared equally baffled and confused. He looked at Mr Fox in amazement. "Did you see that?" he said. "All them tyres gone darn at once!"

"How could that happen?" said Mr Fox, goggling at the new caretaker with a mixture of suspicion and astonishment.

Ron scratched his head. "Search me, guv," he said. "Could it be the particular balance – what wiv' Tyson in the back, not to mention that very large quantity of gay and frisky sitting there as well, combined with the gravelly texture of the road? Or them godfers of yours put glass on the drive? Nah! More like a built-in designer fault organized by the valve industry. You leave it to me, guv. I'll fix it, once I've got my things sorted."

To be fair to Ron, he got down to work straight away – but from the moment he arrived there always seemed to be more work to be done.

For instance, as Mr Fox entered his study, his door sprang off its hinges and fell flat into the corridor. It was a mercy no one was out there at the time or they would have been killed. And while Mr Roy, the geography teacher, was unpacking, a pane of glass in his room suddenly shattered.

Mrs Grain, the Latin teacher, was amazed, while she was writing out the new term's timetable in the common room, to find that a whole strip of wallpaper uncurled itself from the top down to the floor, and lay in a sinister roll at her feet. Miss Shepherd, the craft and cookery teacher, found all the drawers of her chest of drawers stuck fast. And Mr Fritz discovered a huge, weird green stain on his bedspread, which he didn't say anything about in case someone accused him of doing scientific experiments in his room. He hadn't, as yet, done any this term, but he didn't want to draw attention to himself. He decided to live with the green stain, even though it was rather smelly.

"Thank goodness we have Ron," said Mr Fox to Mr Fritz in his study over a drink later that evening. "Heavens knows how old Crumbly would have coped. Crumbly was so useless and he never maintained anything. These are all things that were just waiting to go wrong. Then the cunning old devil has a heart attack just as he's required to do an honest day's work for once in his life."

There was rather an ominous silence from Mr Fritz, who obviously didn't really go along with this theory.

"So – er – what do you think of Ron?" asked Mr Fox rather nervously.

Mr Fritz looked at the headmaster with a beady eye. "Well, I suppose he's better than nothing," he said. "And you did have to get him in a hurry. But I can't say I…"

"I know, I know," said Mr Fox. "But there was really no alternative."

"What's his other name?"

"Grunt," said Mr Fox, sheepishly. "Not a very prepossessing name, I agree. But you can't judge a caretaker by his name."

"What are his references like?" said Mr Fritz suspiciously. He had a strong feeling that Mr Fox had failed to get any.

"Oh, I'm following them up," said Mr Fox, unwilling to admit that Fritz's unspoken fears were correct. "At least he's cheap. And agrees to be paid in cash, thus circumventing any tax problems. No point in putting him through the books. Only get the Inland Revenue after us for contributions."

"There is a rumour," said Mr Fritz, rather disapprovingly, "that he has a dog. A rather vicious dog."

"Lucy," said Mr Fox. It all suddenly sounded most implausible. But he didn't want to tell Mr Fritz about Lucy's real name. "I agree – that is a problem. But he has assured me that he will keep him – I mean her – locked up. And that if there is any trouble he will leave immediately."

Mr Fritz looked at Mr Fox and shook his head. "I hope you know what you're doing, headmaster," he said. "Anyway, let's hope for the best. It's only temporary after all, isn't it?"

"My own thoughts exactly," said Mr Fox, relieved. "And now, let's have another drink. The day before the beginning of term is always taxing, isn't it?"

He reached for the whisky bottle but, as he was about to pour, the bottle exploded in his hand.

*   *   *

Tom and Miles shared a room and had already
unpacked. Because they'd been too late for
supper, they'd scrounged quite a nice little
picnic of hard-boiled eggs and water biscuits
and ice-cream from the kitchens and were
eating it in their room. Susan had joined them
from her room across the corridor which she
shared with Sheila, who was mad about ballet.

"I didn't like the look of that new caretaker,
did you?" she said, sweeping hard-boiled
eggshell into the wastepaper basket. Tom was
showing Miles the new Gameboy he'd got for
his birthday, and his book, *Great Mysteries of
the World*, and Miles was in the middle of
demonstrating a conjuring trick from a set his
dad had bought him as a going-back-to-school
present. "Oh, do put it away for a minute
won't you," she begged Tom as the Gameboy
bleeped and squeaked.

Tom sighed as he put it down. "You're
worse than my mother," he said. "But I agree
with you about Ron. He had a distinct air of –
well, he was kind of threatening."

"He's a male chauvinist pig," said Susan,
disapproving.

"You're telling me," said Tom, searching for
his pyjama cord and discovering it wrapped
soggily round a damp flannel in his sponge-
bag. "Did you see his arms? As he was going
into reverse, his sleeve pulled up a bit and I saw

29

a naked lady tattooed on his wrist."

"Ugh!" said Susan.

"Oooh!" said Miles eagerly. "That's what I'll get done when I'm older. Then I'll never be alone!"

"Miles!" said Susan, throwing a pillow at him. "Do you never think of anything else?"

"Rarely," said Miles, dodging the pillow. "You wait, Tom and I will soon be spending all our days down in Ron's little caretaking room discussing the ladies."

"I don't think we will," said Tom, smiling. "He's got a horrible dog, too. Mr Carstairs told me."

"How do you know it's horrible?" said Susan. "It might be a sweet little poodle. On second thoughts, there's no way that man could have a sweet little poodle."

"No, Mr Carstairs knows a horrible dog when he sees one," said Miles. "He says this is a mixture of every horrible breed you can imagine – pit bull, Alsatian, Rottweiler, Dobermann pinscher..."

"Lion, vulture, werewolf..." added Tom.

"Probably got a touch of Miles and Tom about it, too," said Susan, laughing. She ducked a cushion as the bell went, signalling it was time for lights out.

The first assembly at school was always a fiasco. Half the pupils were late having forgotten something, rummaging around in their suitcases to find lost ties, school shoes, the new jacket rather than last year's old tiny one that seemed to have been packed by mistake and so on. The teachers were organizing last-minute timetables, counting text books, discussing curricula and comparing notes – and the last thing they wanted was to attend assembly. But eventually everyone crowded into the vast hall, chattering and gossiping until Mr Fox roared for silence.

He stepped forward on the podium, wearing the threadbare black gown he always wore at both the beginning and end of term, a dark silhouette against the stained glass window behind. It showed, in reds and greens, the figure of Burlap Hall's great Victorian founder, Mr Septimus Burlap, pointing with a cane to plans for the Hall itself. Underneath, in green glass letters, were the words NOLITE IGNARI ESSE – meaning "Do not be ignorant". Or, as Miles always said, "Don't be a wally."

The headmaster started to speak. He talked of the importance of punctuality, of good manners, of the pupils putting their backs to the wheel and then he read out a list of monitors. Much to Miles' fury he had been made one that term. ("Slave labour," he whispered to Tom.)

Then he talked sadly of Mr Crumbly's illness and announced that Mr Grunt would be temporarily taking his place. A murmur ran through the school. Rumour of Ron Grunt's unusual looks and unpleasant ways had already taken hold – and everyone felt rather threatened by his presence.

It was just after this announcement, with a flourish of a flapping black arm, that Mr Fox signalled to Signor Ruzzi, the wild Italian music teacher, to start the school anthem. The teachers behind him rose from their chairs. And Signor Ruzzi lifted his hands.

But as he brought them down onto the keys, there was what seemed like a gigantic crack of lightning. And down the stained glass window behind Mr Fox appeared an enormous split, cracking from the top of the top-hatted head of the Victorian founder right down to the E of ESSE.

There was pandemonium in the hall. Everyone clutched each other, panic-stricken. What on earth was happening?

"Tom!" whispered Susan, seizing his arm and trembling violently. "What's going on?"

"I don't know," said Tom. "But frankly," he added darkly, "I don't like the look of it. I don't like the look of it at all."

CHAPTER TWO

The phenomenon was inexplicable. It hadn't been caused by a flash of lightning. There had been no sudden vibration from a faraway explosion. One minute everyone was stifling with boredom in the stuffy old assembly hall as Mr Fox droned on; the next the stained glass was split from top to bottom, pupils were screaming and the air was crackling with fear.

"Freak electrical currents" was the feeble excuse that Mr Fritz came up with. And even he didn't believe it. But he did start making a private list of all the strange events that were occurring. And during the next few days, his list became alarmingly long.

There was the geography lesson with Mr Roy. It had all started perfectly normally. Mr Roy was his usual white-faced and under-nourished self – he was a vegetarian who kept a pot of sunflower seeds on his desk to pick at when he felt nervous or hungry. He announced that this term they were going to study Ordnance Survey maps.

Miles groaned. "If there's one thing I hate," he said, under his breath, "it's Ordnance Survey maps." He said it in a way that made him sound as if he'd been dogged by the subject since birth.

"What are they?" whispered Tom.

"Heaven knows," said Miles. "But don't they just sound like the most boring things in the world?"

Mr Roy was drawing weird circles on the board in chalk and explaining how the rings each represented a different height – "all lines being referred to the datum line, which is twelve and a half feet below the Trinity High-water mark and four and a half feet above the Trinity Low-water mark."

Miles gave a deep sigh and Mr Roy whirled round.

"Miles! Are you paying attention?" he said, reaching for the sunflower seeds.

"Yes, sir," said Miles, trying not to smirk.

"Well, come up here and start drawing some lines. Here is a mountain that I am drawing on the board and I want you to translate this mountain into an Ordnance Survey representation of it." He put the chalk in a little dish by the blackboard, sat down at his desk and seized his sunflower seeds again.

And then a most extraordinary thing happened. The chalk rose in mid-air and started drawing, by itself, on the board. And it didn't draw an Ordnance Survey map of a mountain. It drew a little round dot at the top of the mountain and then continued down the mountain, along, drawing two long legs and feet, then continued back on itself with a curvaceous bottom, along to the head of a luscious-looking blonde, down to her neck and along to join the other side of the mountain. Drawn on the board was not a mountain, in Ordnance Survey terms, but a huge naked lady. Miles stopped in his tracks while the rest of the class tried to stifle their giggles.

"What are you laughing at?" said Mr Roy fiercely. Then he turned round and saw what was on the board.

"Miles!" he said, shocked. "How dare you! Rub that out at once! And you will have detention instead of tea this afternoon!"

"But, sir, it wasn't me!" protested Miles, genuinely indignant.

"Well, I'd like to know who it was then," said Mr Roy, snatching the cloth from the top of the blackboard and scrubbing out the picture himself.

"It wasn't him!" roared the class. "It was the chalk! It did it by itself!"

Mr Roy turned round. "Rubbish!" he said.

But as he spoke, so his pot of sunflower seeds rose up off the desk and hovered in front of his face. The geography teacher started back. His fishy little eyes bulged. A spot of colour came to his wan cheeks. The pot remained in mid-air. Tentatively, Mr Roy extended a white hand and checked all round the pot for hidden strings. Nothing. The pot then rose above Mr Roy sharply and swiftly tipped its contents over his head.

"Miles!" shouted Mr Roy. "I shall report you to Mr Fox at once!"

"But it wasn't him, sir!" said Asquith Minor, loyally putting up his hand.

"So who was it?" said Mr Roy, thoroughly shaken and staring at the empty pot of sunflower seeds. "Asquith Minor?"

"No, sir," said Asquith Minor. "It seemed as if it was, well, magic."

Mr Roy glowered and sat down. "This time we'll forget all about it. Some freak of the atmosphere. Most curious. Now, let's start again. Perhaps *you* can make an Ordnance Survey representation of this mountain, Asquith Minor?"

He hid his embarrassment by leafing over the pages of the latest issue of the Lanchester Geographical Society's magazine. "'Crop farming, Jute and Tundra,'" he read. And settled down to a nice browse.

The next weird phenomenon occurred when

Mrs Grain came in to teach them about Caesar's Gallic Wars.

"Good morning, class!" intoned Mrs Grain, as she came in. "Or, as Caesar would say: 'Salute!'"

"Good morning, Mrs Grain," mumbled the class.

"Today and for the rest of this term we will be studying the Gallic Wars."

"Not the Gallic Wars!" wailed Miles, quietly. "If there's one thing I can't stand it's the Gallic Wars!"

Tom was going to ask him what it was, but remembered the answer he got to the Ordnance Survey maps so kept his mouth shut.

Mrs Grain sat down. "Now, before we start I'm going to tell you a little bit about Caesar himself. He was born on the twelfth of July in the year 100 BC. A long time ago. He was assassinated in 44 BC after becoming emperor of Rome.

Sheila put up her hand. "How could he be assassinated before he was born?" she asked.

"Or was he born when he was sixty and assassinated when he was six!" tittered Asquith Minor.

Mrs Grain drummed her fingers. "BC, if you didn't know, is 'before Christ'. Therefore the numbers go backwards, like negative numbers, until Christ was born."

Everyone in the class looked rather baffled.

("I like the idea of Caesar fighting the Gallic Wars in his nappies, don't you?" whispered Miles.)

Mrs Grain tapped on her desk. "But he was best known for his exploits as a soldier and a –" at this moment two of Mrs Grain's hairpins rose from her head and a great lock of thin brown hair fell onto her shoulder; she put her hand to her head "– and a conqueror of other nations. Indeed, Caesar not only conquered Gaul but also –" the two pins landed on the desk but meanwhile another two pins detached themselves from the other side of her head and more hair fell down; Sheila started to laugh as Mrs Grain fumbled with the two original pins and replaced them – "but also England. Our language is influenced by the Latin that the great Caesar brought to…"

At this point the next couple of pins landed on Mrs Grain's desk as two of her combs detached themselves, leaving her hair tumbling down her back. She looked most peculiar. Tom had once seen Mrs Grain on her way to the bathroom at night and had mistaken her for a ghost with her long trailing hair. It looked so different when she had it pinned in place. Desperately, Mrs Grain fumbled with her hair. But the faster she replaced the pins and combs in her hair, the faster the magical presence removed them and replaced them on the desk in front of her.

It was highly amusing. But nothing like as funny as what happened at lunchtime. Mr Fox always stood to say grace – but this time, as he was speaking, the chair behind him was simply dragged away by invisible hands. The entire school goggled. What would happen next? It was inevitable. Mr Fox sat down, with a loud yell, on his bottom, on the floor, cursing and swearing and searching around for the miserable boy or girl who'd wreaked this trick on him.

It was curious that no one could quite believe that it *wasn't* some pupil who was behind it all. Over lunch everyone was saying: "Who did it?" "How did they do it?" "Was there a concealed string?" and so on. Even Susan wouldn't entertain Tom's and Miles' doubts when they confided in her.

"Rubbish," she said. "You're always thinking things are supernatural or something funny's going on."

"And we're always right!" said Miles, passing her a jug of custard. "Remember Mr Culard – and the phantom!"*

"But all that was a long time ago," said Susan. "You've seen magic shows on telly. This is just someone come back from the holidays with a magic kit." She looked hard at Miles.

But as she took the custard, the jug gave a

*Vampire Master and Phantom of Burlap Hall

shake, lifted itself up in the air and, with a little tip like a curtsy, poured a small trickle of yellow liquid on Susan's frizzy hair.

"So what do you think now?" said Miles, producing a handkerchief and seizing the jug. But Susan was too astonished to speak.

The mysterious happenings didn't only occur indoors, either. After lunch Mr Carstairs organized the usual run over the lawn, down to the spinney, up by the brook and round by the village and back.

"Come on, kids!" he yelled, jumping up and down and waggling his hands in a "I'm-a-fit-person-and-I'm-going-to-be-relaxed" kind of way. "Race you all! Ready, steady, go!"

Everyone ran off over the lawn – everyone, that is, except Mr Carstairs. Mr Carstairs suddenly fell over on the gravel at the starting line. Turning, Tom saw the teacher sprawled on the ground, red-faced and flushed. He ran back. "Are you all right, sir?" he asked. "Oh, your knees are bleeding! What happened? Did you trip?" Mr Carstairs brushed the gravel from his face as he struggled to his feet. Then he looked down at his shoes. He saw something extraordinary. The laces on his two trainers had been tied together in an extremely tight knot.

"Sir!" said Tom. "How did that happen?"

"Exactly!" said Mr Carstairs, getting out a handkerchief and wiping the blood from his knees before sitting down and untying his laces. "How indeed? Because only seconds before I took my first step I was jumping up and down and jogging on the spot. It's – it's sinister, this."

It was at this point that they heard a great growling and panting and an enormous black dog appeared – apparently from nowhere. It had green eyes and huge teeth and it took one look at Mr Carstairs' bloody knee and started to bark furiously.

"Watch out! He smells blood, sir," cried Tom, pulling the teacher to his feet. As the dog bared its teeth and prepared to leap on Mr Carstairs, a rough voice could be heard through the bushes. "Tyson! Tyson! Down, down!" And suddenly Ron Grunt appeared, gasping. He seized the dog by the scruff of its neck and pulled it away. Taking a chain from his pocket, he tied it harshly round the dog's neck.

"Sorry, abart the cherry, sir," he said, apologetically. "Tys – I mean, er, Lucy – can sometimes be a bit aggressive. But I'm always on his – I mean her – tail. So never you fear. She wouldn't have hurt you, sir. Lovely with godfers."

Tyson was growling ferociously all the time Ron was talking, while Ron delivered fierce kicks to get the dog to sit down.

"What do you mean, cherry?" said Mr Carstairs. "I thought she was called Lucy."

"Cherry Hogg, dog," said Ron, leering up at the English teacher. "So what's happened to yer I suppose? And," he added, looking down, "yer biscuits, then?"

"I suppose? Biscuits?" said Mr Carstairs.

"I suppose, nose. And biscuits and cheese, knees – it's rhymin'—"

"Never mind!" snapped Mr Carstairs. "Firstly that dog should be kept on a lead at all times. Secondly it looks like one of those breeds that needs a muzzle. And thirdly," he added, staring hard at the dog, "if that dog's a girl, I'm the Queen Mother."

Ron scratched his head. "Queen Mother?" he said, in a puzzled way. "Mother? Brother? Other? You're not the Queen Mother, mate, I can assure you of that. Oh, er, a joke!" he said. "Oh, and abart, er, Lucy. Well, aha, well spotted, sir. No, she's not a girl. I mean he's not a bird. He's a bloke."

"Of course he's not a bird," said Mr Carstairs getting confused. "He's a dog. Or a cherry. Oh, for heaven's sake, you know what I mean."

"I do indeed, sir," said Ron. "No, we made a mistake at birth. Called him Lucy. Just a little joke."

"Didn't you call him something else just now, anyway?" said Mr Carstairs, looking at Ron suspiciously. "Like Tyson?"

Ron looked uncomfortable. "Maybe," he

said, cautiously. "But look at that biscuit, sir. Need some antiseptic on that, I'll be bound. I'll get the first-aid kit. This school!" he added, shaking his head. "Talk abart accident-prone. I don't know I'd have taken this job on if I'd known. You don't need just one caretaker 'ere, guv, you need abart a country cousin. Dozen," he added helpfully as he disappeared with his dog into the bushes.

"Tyson!" said Mr Carstairs to Tom, angrily. "What a name for a dog! I don't like that man at all, I can tell you. I can't think why Mr Fox employed him. More things have gone wrong since the day he arrived than ever went wrong in Mr Crumbly's entire lifetime."

"We've run out of ingredients!" wailed Miss Shepherd. She had been weighing out flour, fat, oil, butter and mushrooms. She'd also been counting onions, peppers and eggs. This term Miss Shepherd was devoting her time to cookery lessons.

"I'm afraid," she said to the assembled class, which was gathered in the huge kitchens of Burlap Hall, still hot, steamy and redolent of the lunch they'd just consumed, "that it will have to be macramé this afternoon instead of cooking."

"Macramé!" said Asquith Minor. "But that would be *disgusting* to eat!"

Miss Shepherd looked at him sharply.

43

"Macramé isn't for eating, it's for making."

"Oh, Miss Shepherd!" moaned Sheila. "Not macramé again! I did so much macramé last term I could hardly play the piano all holidays my fingers were in such knots."

"Not macramé!" whispered Miles. "If there's one thing I hate, it's macramé."

If there was one thing Tom hated too it was macramé. So he put up his hand. "If you give me a list I'll run down to the village and get any extra ingredients, Miss Shepherd," he said. "I'm sure you've got enough for at least *some* stuff to cook, haven't you?"

"Oh, Tom!" said Miss Shepherd gratefully, wiping the drip from the end of her nose. The class breathed a communal sigh of relief. It was never nice cooking with Miss Shepherd when she had a drip on the end of her nose. Everyone always got very anxious when she bent over the pastry. "But you'll be over-taxing yourself, dear. You've just been on a run!"

"No, I was looking after Mr Carstairs, who fell," said Tom. "I'd welcome some fresh air!"

"Excellent," said Miss Shepherd, writing a list. "Because macramé didn't sound too popular, did it, boys and girls?"

She gave the list and some money to Tom. And as he left he heard her saying, "Quiche Lorraine, boys and girls. Not as easy to make as you might think! We only have enough ingredients for two, so until Tom returns, some will have to watch while the others cook."

Tom struggled into his coat, got his bike from the barn where they were all stacked, and set off for the village. Then he remembered: it was Thursday – early-closing day in the village. He'd have to go into Lanchester. He looked at his watch. He could get there with ten minutes' hard cycling and then it would be another ten minutes' shopping and ten minutes back again. True, the lesson would be nearly over when he returned, but who cared? If there was one thing he hated more than macramé, it was quiche Lorraines – horrible slimy things with soggy pastry bottoms.

He had a very pleasant bike ride, parked his machine and got his provisions from Tesco. Looking at his watch, he saw he was in good time and could afford to dawdle. He looked in the window of the computer shop and wished he could afford another Gameboy. He stared at the records in Our Price and checked out the charts. Then he peered into a rather horrible men's clothes shop and decided that all the clothes were too naff even to consider. And then he hurried back to his bike.

But as he was walking, he passed the bus shelter. His steps became slower. This must be where Lanchester Larry was found murdered. Tom shivered a bit. Poor old Lanchester Larry. Never did anyone any harm. He wondered who his family was or if he even had any. He paused in front of a large poster stuck up on the side of the shelter.

"MURDER!" it said. "Can you help? On January 9th a vagrant, known locally as Lanchester Larry, was found fatally stabbed in this bus shelter. Did you see anything? If so, please ring Lanchester Police Station." Next to it was a poster with a very bad drawing of a face on it. And next to the drawing was the outline of a large black dog. Underneath both drawings was printed: "Have you seen this man or his dog? We would like to eliminate him from our enquiries."

Tom's mind reeled. A dreadful idea had taken hold. It was the black dog that did it! How could he have forgotten? It had all been in the newspaper report. No wonder Ron Grunt gave them all the creeps. Could it possibly be that Ron Grunt was none other than the murderer of Lanchester Larry?

As Tom cycled back to Burlap Hall, his carrier-bag of mushrooms, onions and flour swinging from his handlebars, he was deep in thought. Certainly the timing was right. As he understood it, Mr Fox had employed Ron Grunt the very day after the murder. And what better place to hide than a school? He would have to tell Miles and Susan. It was all very frightening.

* * *

Miss Shepherd was just getting the quiches out of the oven when Tom dashed through the door. She looked up, oven gloves at the ready. "Oh, Tom, you've missed everything!" she said.

"I had to go to Lanchester, I'm afraid," said Tom.

"What a noble boy," said Miss Shepherd, going back to the oven. "I just hope you didn't catch cold. You shall have an especially large piece of quiche as a reward."

Miles stuck his finger down his throat in a puking sign as Miss Shepherd leaned down to open the oven door. But she had barely turned the handle when the door banged wide and from the oven, like a couple of rockets, came the quiches. They shot out, whizzed up to the ceiling, and then, in a kind of mocking dance, they bounced in the air out of the room and into the corridor.

"Good heavens!" cried Miss Shepherd.

"Let's catch them!" shouted Susan. And the whole class rushed out after the errant quiches that were now bobbing through the main door and into the garden. Up and up they flew, through the trees, until eventually they were just specks in the sky. Everyone stared after them.

"And they smelt rather good," said Miles, slightly wistfully. "What a pity. The only chance I get to taste a bit of quiche I actually fancy and it disappears."

"You don't believe it could have been the lightness of the pastry, do you?" said Sheila, panting. She'd followed the quiches further and now returned, red in the face.

Tom rushed up, just in time to see the quiches vanishing, like a pair of tiny flying saucers, over the brow of a hill. "Quiches are by their nature leaden and stodgy," he said. "No, it's another of these weird happenings at work."

"What weird happenings?" asked Sheila.

"All these things. You know, Mr Fox and the chair, the chalk in Mr Roy's class..." said Asquith Minor.

"You don't think it could be some electrical current at work?" said Susan, rather vaguely.

"Or maybe we're on a ley line," said Miles.

"What's a ley line?" asked Susan.

"Oh, I don't know. It's meant to be some kind of line with magical powers from the days of the Druids. For instance, if you draw a line between Stonehenge and, say, Glastonbury, which is full of old remains, the extraordinary thing is, it's absolutely straight."

"Of course it's straight, you nerd," said Tom. "There are only two points. No, I think something else is at work here." Then he lowered his voice so Sheila and Asquith Minor couldn't hear. "And do you know, I think it's all tied up, in some way, with Ron Grunt."

Hearing Tom whispering, Asquith Minor sidled up. "What are you on about?" he said.

"Nothing," said Tom airily, walking away. But when he saw Miles later on he said, "Let's all meet after supper down in the spinney and I'll tell you what I think. I don't want to be overheard."

That evening Mr Fox held his usual beginning-of-term meeting for the staff, delayed owing to all the extraordinary events of the past few days. It was normally an amiable affair, with holiday snaps exchanged, general pleasantries and only a little time for discussion about future plans. Tempers were usually not yet frayed; everyone was in a good mood. But this particular meeting was different. Although only a week had gone by, Mr Fox could sense a different atmosphere from usual. There was a tension and anxiety in the air. "Pessimissimus!" he sighed to himself.

Some things were the same as ever. Signor Ruzzi had, as usual, pinched the most comfortable chair; he even left a sheet of music on it to reserve it for himself when he jumped up to attend to the disgusting coffee he was brewing on the other side of the room.

"Just a spot," Mr Fox said graciously, as the music teacher offered him the first cup. "A little of your delicious coffee goes a very, very long way."

Mrs Grain sniffed. "Wonderful smell!" she said. "Reminds me of Italy. No doubt it's what the remarkable Julius Caesar drank in the praetors' triumvirate."

Mr Carstairs came in with Miss Shepherd. He had a plaster on his nose and he was limping.

"How did you get that?" asked Mr Roy, who had been there all along, but had been lurking nervously in the shadows.

"I'll explain later," said Mr Carstairs rather grimly. "Under 'other business'."

Mr Fox groaned inside. Coffee was handed round. Mr Fritz, as usual, arrived late and smelling of a mixture of pipe-smoke and sulphuric acid (Mr Fox made a mental note to have a word with him about doing experiments in his room). And then, after giving his coffee a token sniff, which alone would reduce his sleeping capacity by about three hours, Mr Fox rose to his feet.

"Welcome back to Burlap Hall," he intoned. "An eventful term, so far, but luckily our electricity is still on despite the pressures from the Board, and I'm delighted to see you."

A few minor details about the timetable were sorted out; Signor Ruzzi complained about the piano – the soft pedal wasn't soft enough apparently. But why he wanted a soft pedal, Mr Fox couldn't work out. It must feel so squishy under his foot. Still that was music teachers for you. He promised to look into it. There was discussion about Parents' Day. And then Mr Carstairs brought up the topic of Ron Grunt's dog.

"I'll certainly see that he – I mean she – is muzzled and kept on a lead," said Mr Fox.

"He," said Mr Carstairs.

"I must say I don't like or trust the man," said Mrs Grain. "He gives me the creeps. I saw him in the woodshed with his sleeves rolled up. And quite honestly, what he's got on his arms! I would have thought that the Indecency Squad could have had him put in prison for the pictures he displays on his biceps alone."

"He's very good at his job," said Mr Fox lamely, hoping he wouldn't have to go too far into the subject of Ron. "And we must all admit he's been kept very busy recently."

"And that brings me to 'any other business'," said Mr Carstairs. "What is the cause of all these goings on? Everywhere I go there seem to be things dancing in the air, or doors coming off hinges or mirrors cracking. Today I was going for a run and found my shoelaces were tied together!"

"Those boys and girls!" murmured Miss Shepherd.

"No, Miss Shepherd, it wasn't those 'boys and girls' as you call them, or 'kids' as I prefer. I have absolutely no idea how it happened at all."

"My bed has broken completely," said Mr Roy. "I didn't like to mention it so early in the term, but last night at four in the morning, all the legs suddenly broke at once. And you know I am not a heavy man." Everyone stared at him. Indeed he was not a heavy man. He was so thin and wispy he hardly made any impression on the cushions in his chair.

"And," said Mrs Grain, "I woke this morning to find a great splash of paint on my wall which wasn't there the night before. Perhaps you could ask Mr Grunt to give it a fresh coat, headmaster. It is very unsightly."

"My room was in a dreadful mess when I got back to it after teaching, yesterday," said Mr Fritz, who had been making detailed notes of all these experiences. "It was as if a burglar had been into it. Complete confusion, a total shambles, clothes everywhere, chairs upturned..."

There was a general silence as everyone thought the same thing. That it sounded exactly as Mr Fritz *always* left his room.

Mr Fox shook his head. "The happenings are all most strange. It is almost as if we are being – well, haunted. I hope you don't think I am being stupid, but I think the best thing to do would be to get the vicar in and ask his advice."

"Evil spirits!" shrieked Miss Shepherd, shrinking into her chair. "Not evil spirits!"

"No, no," said Mr Fritz. "Just a happy precaution. Good idea."

"Because," said Mr Fox, "I quite agree. Something must be done!"

After supper Tom, Miles and Susan met down in the bushes beyond the lawn. They squatted in the shadow of a rhododendron bush while Tom told them of his suspicions.

"I know there's no proof," he concluded, rather weakly. "But it's just a feeling in my bones."

"You didn't get a copy of the picture, did you?" said Miles. "Then we could compare it to Ron."

"No, and it would make no difference anyway. All those Identikit pictures look the same. And, anyway, I may be jumping to conclusions."

"Look – this is just another thought. But do you think they're connected – the weird happenings and Ron?" asked Susan, carefully shaking a woodlouse from her skirt onto the grass. It scampered through a patch of fading sunlight before disappearing under a pile of leaves.

Tom wrinkled his brow as he thought. "Could be," he said, eventually. "He's a caretaker. He wants to keep his job. I think he's making as many odd things as possible happen so that he's kept busy. And if he wrecks enough of the school then Mr Fox will need him so much he might keep him on even after Mr Crumbly's returned. And the other thing that puzzles me is that all these weird things happen to everyone except Ron. Isn't that odd?"

Miles looked dubious. "I can understand that being the reason for the door of Mr Fox's study breaking ... and the window," said Miles. "But not all these things dancing about in the air. I mean flying quiches aren't going to make Ron's job any more secure, are they?"

"That's what I can't work out," said Tom, shaking his head.

"I think we ought to test him," said Tom.

"But wouldn't that be a bit dangerous?" said Miles.

"If he *is* a murderer?" said Susan.

"We'll just have to think of a way," said Tom. And then there was a grunting and rustling noise. Through the bushes pushed a big wet doggy nose – Tyson himself. Susan gave a little shriek and jumped up – because hot on the dog's heels was none other than Ron Grunt.

Tom and Miles both hurried to their feet. The caretaker stopped and stared at them, an unpleasant gleam in his eyes. Barefoot and muscular, he looked like an evil dwarf.

"What you doin'?" he said menacingly.

"Just having a chat," said Susan. "It's a free country."

"Hmm," said the caretaker. He pushed up his sleeves, revealing, on the left arm, a blue lion grappling with a snake and, on the right, a bikini-clad lady apparently dancing with a skeleton. He scratched his nose with a filthy fingernail. Tom noticed letters tattooed on his knuckles: "TOL." on one hand and "RUBE" on the other. "Free for some. Can I give you a bit of advice, lads?"

Tom and Miles nodded, the colour draining from their faces. Had he heard what they'd been saying? The prospect was too terrifying to contemplate.

Ron was linking his fingers together as if he were praying. Then he pushed his knuckles towards the three friends.

"I don't know if you can read," he said rudely. "But if I were you I wouldn't go looking for this." Staring, Tom saw that his interlinked knuckles now read "TROUBLE.".

"I don't know what you were talking abart," said the caretaker. "And maybe you were just discussing something you seen on the custard and jelly. If by any chance you weren't, then if I were you I'd keep me north and souths shut." There was a sinister pause. "Or you might find you get my oliver rammed down your throats. Unnerstand?"

Despite not understanding each word that he was saying, his general drift was clear enough. Tom and Miles gulped and nodded.

Ron unlaced his hands, gave them all another piercing look, whistled to his dog, and disappeared into the bushes. Tom's heart was thumping in his chest.

"Do you think he heard?" he whispered.

Miles shrugged. "I don't think he quite knows what he heard. But I suspect he suspects we suspect, if you see what I mean."

"And that's quite bad enough," said Tom gloomily, as they walked back to the school.

CHAPTER THREE

"I wonder if he'll walk round the school holding a cross and sprinkling holy water over everything," said Miles thoughtfully. He was thinking about the vicar – rumours of his arrival had spread like wildfire.

"He'd better not try sprinkling holy water over me," said Asquith Minor, stuffing his sweaty gear into a plastic bag and hanging it up on a hook. Burlap Hall had just lost a game of cricket to St Beowulf's.

"No. Being an evil spirit, you might well disappear," said Tom, grinning.

"Oh, thanks!" said Asquith Minor. "But if he's after evil spirits, the first to go would be Mr Fox."

"And that new caretaker, Ron," added Tom.

"Yes!" said Asquith Minor, searching for his

school trousers. "He gives me the creeps. He's always lurking in the bushes."

"He goes there to roll up his sleeves and flex his muscles so he can see his disgusting tattoos in action," said Miles.

"I saw him in his shed the other day," said Asquith Minor, "and when I waved at him through his window he got absolutely furious and stormed out shaking his fist and telling me I'd get a punch on the Hampsteads if I didn't leave him on his Jack."

"Hampsteads?" said Tom.

"Hampstead – er – Heath?" said Miles.

"Teeth!" said Asquith Minor, looking a bit pale as he realized what it meant. "And Jack Jones means alone."

"What was he doing?" asked Tom, curious.

"That's what was so funny," said Asquith Minor. "You'd think he'd be repotting bulbs, or soldering bits of metal or whatever care-takers do. But he seemed to be collecting bits of paper and putting them in a folder. It was really weird. When he saw me looking, he pushed them out of sight and that's when he came out and threatened me."

"Perhaps he was writing his autobiogra-phy," suggested Miles, rather sarcastically.

"Or sorting out his tax," said Tom, pulling a wry face.

"Oh, yeah?" said Asquith Minor, finding his trousers at last and pulling them on. "It didn't look like that to me."

Tom looked at Miles and they gave each other a meaningful nod. Then they all went back to the school for tea.

The vicar's visit didn't end until eleven o'clock. He irritated Mr Fox by trying to explain the Holy Ghost to him, not to mention most of the Bible, but was eventually persuaded to go round the school exorcizing the place by sprinkling holy water about the classrooms and muttering curious incantations that put any passing pupil into fits of giggles.

It was dark when the good man left and Tom and Miles, craning out of their bedroom window, overheard Mr Fox saying goodbye to him.

"A thousand thanks, my dear vicar," said Mr Fox, shaking him by the hand. "I have no doubt these unpleasant happenings will stop now. I am eternally grateful to you."

"God bless you," said the vicar, hopping onto his bicycle. "And remember what I told you about the Three in One."

"Indeed, indeed – makes four," replied Mr Fox cheerfully as he waved at the vicar's dark shape cycling down the drive, whistling. From their window, Tom and Miles could see the top of Mr Fox's bald head as he watched the vicar get smaller in the distance. Then the headmaster turned to go back into the school.

But, as he did so, there was a creaking noise. The front door seemed to be heaving at its hinges. Then, with a ripping sound, it broke free and leapt into the night air, landing, with a crash, in the bushes.

"Oh, oh, oh, pessimissimus!" wailed Mr Fox. "I can't bear it." And he went indoors.

"That was extraordinary!" said Tom to Miles. "What on earth's going on?"

But as Miles was about to reply, the central light in their room exploded, the bulb shattering into a thousand tiny shards.

"I think we ought to ask Mr Fritz what he thinks," said Susan, at breakfast. She'd had her own unpleasant experiences the night before. While she was asleep, all the bedclothes had been pulled off her at three in the morning. She had found them mysteriously and neatly folded in a drawer when she'd woken, freezing.

"He's always been helpful in the past," said Miles.

"Well, come on," said Tom. "What are we waiting for?" He looked at his watch. "We'll just catch him."

They caught Mr Fritz, who was actually trying to catch something else. His pyjamas were floating in the air and he was jumping up to grasp them so he could stuff them under his pillow. When the three knocked he told them

to come in, but to open the door only a crack
– "in case my pyjamas fly out."

"Well, what can I do for you?" said Mr
Fritz, folding up his pyjamas as they entered.
"Sit down, sit down. Is it a science problem?
Or is the destruction of the ozone layer con-
fusing you? Many pupils this term seem con-
cerned about the future of this planet and what
I always say is…"

"No," said Tom quickly. He didn't want to
get Mr Fritz on to the ozone layer. "It's about
these, er, happenings."

Mr Fritz looked more serious. He sat down
in a very baggy, old armchair, took out his pipe
and lit it.

"They've been worrying me, too," he said.
"But I rather hoped the vicar would put an end
to it all."

"But he hasn't, has he?" said Tom. "Just
after he'd gone, the school door pulled itself
off its hinges and flew into the air. And our
light bulb exploded. And Susan's bedclothes
came off."

"All explicable," said Mr Fritz. "In theory,
at least."

"Then what about your pyjamas, sir?" said
Miles boldly. "What were you talking about
when you said you didn't want them to fly out
of the room?"

Mr Fritz hesitated. He didn't want to
frighten them. Then he nodded. "Yes, my pyja-

mas were, indeed, flying around," he confessed. "But I still feel it might be something to do with freak electrical currents combined with a lowering of pressure and the time of the year. It could, indeed, have something to do with the ozone layer!" he added hopefully. At least he was on home territory with the ozone layer. He hated being faced with pupils and unable to answer their questions. It made him feel inadequate.

Susan looked at him quizzically. "Come on, sir!" she said. "You're a scientist. You know that's not likely."

Mr Fritz scratched his head. "No, it's not likely," he said. "It's interesting. But you're right. Nothing similar has ever been recorded. But there's always a first time. However…" He lapsed into silence. "I'll be frank."

"OK, Frank," said Miles automatically.

Mr Fritz smiled. He had a nice smile, thought Tom, noticing his lively, twinkling eyes; particularly nice considering he must have heard the joke a thousand times before. "I've been very worried about these events myself. And all I can think that might be responsible is a poltergeist."

"A poltergeist?" said Susan. "What's that?"

"You know, poltergeists," said Miles. "They're – they're – well, things that throw things across rooms and upturn tables and – and – yes, that must be it!" he said.

"But what makes a poltergeist?" asked Tom. "And how do you stop it?"

"As far as I know, in all the recorded cases," said Mr Fritz, "they have only occurred when there are adolescent children around. That is the current theory, anyway. The energy released by children, particularly girls, growing up at this time, seems to spark off strange happenings around them. Just the sort of curious events we've been experiencing here."

Everyone looked at Susan rather oddly.

"Well, don't look at me!" she said furiously. "I may be growing up, but I can assure you I'm not producing poltergeist happenings! I've got better things to do with my energy!"

"Of course you have, my dear," said Mr Fritz hastily. "And that's only one theory. I feel sure that there must be other explanations."

But as he sat in his big, fat armchair, with all the stuffing coming out of the arms, he didn't look very reassuring. And as he looked into the three worried faces he shook his head.

"It's no good theorizing, is it?" he said. "I must go and find the facts. And look into the up-to-date research on the subject."

"Where will you find out?" asked Miles.

"I have heard there is a Royal Institute of Poltergeists in London," said Mr Fritz. "I shall start there. In fact, if I can get some time off, I'll go this weekend."

*　　　*　　　*

Mr Fox was not in a good mood when Mr Fritz tapped on his door and asked for a word. He had just opened his filing cabinet to look for his bottle of whisky and found it wasn't there. Not only was it not there, but all the papers in the PARENTS-WHO-ARE-SLOW-PAYERS file had been muddled up with the papers in the file marked EXAMINATION MARKS PAST, PRESENT AND FUTURE. A bottle of ink had mysteriously spilled, in front of his eyes, onto his desk, and while he was surveying the damage, a brick had come flying in through his window, spraying glass everywhere and narrowly missing his bald head. Mr Fox was not pleased. He was also rather frightened.

"Thank heavens you're here, Fritz!" he cried. "What on earth are we going to do? The school seems to have a curse on it! And that fool vicar has had no effect whatsoever. He just came in, drank my whisky, sprinkled water, which he claimed was holy, over everything and staggered off on his bike! *And* I gave him a fiver towards the church roof! It's a scandal!"

Mr Fritz sat down. "Calm down, headmaster, he said, pulling out his pipe. "I think I have the answer."

"You do?" said Mr Fox wildly, staring at him over his desk. He sat down. "Ouch!" he said. He leaped up and goggled down at the chair. "So that's where it is," he said angrily.

He pulled the whisky bottle from the chair and poured himself a drink.

"Right. What's the answer?"

"I have a feeling that it is a poltergeist," said Mr Fritz.

"A what? A pollyghost?" said Mr Fox. "Come on, pull yourself together, man. You're a scientist not a mystic. Have you no better explanation than that?"

Mr Fritz shook his head sadly, drawing on his pipe. Mr Fox shrank back, waiting nervously for the poisonous exhalation that he knew would follow.

"Only a poltergeist would behave in this way," said Mr Fritz, after breathing pipe-smoke into the headmaster's eyes. "A poltergeist is cheeky, mischievous, and sometimes downright dangerous. Everything points to it. Flying objects, disruptions, stupid pranks…"

"But how can we get rid of it?" asked Mr Fox desperately.

"There is a theory that poltergeists are associated in some way with adolescent children, particularly girls. The energy they release as they are growing up causes some curious energy in the air…"

"Right! We'll get rid of them, then," said Mr Fox, going to his file and looking up the one marked PUPILS: GIRLS. "Confound it!" he cried as he pulled out a bunch of bills. "This pollyghost has been at my filing system – which was never very much in the first place, to be honest." He riffled through the files until he found the papers in a section marked SCHOOL MEALS.

"Poltergeist, not pollyghost," said Mr Fritz. "But anyway, headmaster, you surely aren't thinking of expelling all the adolescent girls? I mean…"

"Of course I am!" said Mr Fox, his nose buried in a sheaf of paperwork. "Now let me see … there's Sheila Patterson, yes, she's one; Sandra Forest, but she's only nine; Avril Boxer, no; Susan Sanders, aha, she's about the right age!" He continued shuffling through his papers and ended up with five sheets of paper – five girls.

"We'll get rid of these girls and, bingo! our problems are over," he said. "I'll write to their parents right now."

"But please don't be so hasty," said Mr Fritz. "It's only a theory! I was hoping to go to London this weekend to find out more about current thinking…"

"Currents, eh? That's an idea. I'll get on to the Electricity Board if this ploy doesn't work," said Mr Fox. "Go off by all means, Fritz. In the meantime I'll get these girls removed as quickly as possible."

"But what will you say? You can't say they're responsible for poltergeists!" said Mr

Fritz. "Oh, do wait till I get back. This could cause no end of trouble. I wish I'd never mentioned it!"

"We've had enough trouble already," said Mr Fox, who, like all weak men, took a strong stand only on issues that were totally inappropriate. "You can't change my mind, Fritz. It all has a ring of truth to it. I can feel it in my bones."

Mr Fritz got up despairingly. "If you say so, headmaster," he said. "But I think you're making a big mistake. Without any real evidence you've no idea what you could be letting yourself in for with these parents, you know."

Mr Fox frowned. He stroked his chin thoughtfully. "You may have a point, Fritz," he said. "I tell you what. I'll ask Ron what he thinks."

"Ron!" said Mr Fritz. "You can't trust him an inch, surely!"

"I appointed him, Fritz," said Mr Fox rather grandly. "He has been totally satisfactory so far. He has worked like a slave repairing all the things that have gone wrong. And remember, he is one person who has access to everyone's quarters – he's in and out of the pupils' rooms repairing things. He is also a man of the world. He is, I think the word is, 'roadworthy'. Unlike some," he said, staring at Mr Fritz to make his point clear.

"I think you mean 'streetwise'," said Mr

Fritz in a low, angry voice.

The headmaster continued. "We've had vicars; you're off to research the pollyghost theory; and what we now need is a new angle on it all, someone with practical experience of life, a hard-headed, down-to-earth, different view of the matter."

"Whatever you say, headmaster," said Mr Fritz wearily. "I'm sure you'll get a 'different' view from Ron. I just dread to think what it is. But I do hope you don't do anything rash when I'm away."

"Rash? Me? Mr Fritz! Surely you know me better than that!" said Mr Fox. And he gave Mr Fritz a hearty pat on the back as he ushered him out of his study.

Ron was busy fixing the net on the tennis court when Mr Fox found him later that afternoon. During the night, despite the fact that there had been not a single gust of wind, the net had mysteriously unhooked itself and become wound round the top of a high chestnut tree. It had taken Ron most of the afternoon to untangle it and he was thoroughly fed up.

"Them godfers, sir!" he complained as he hammered angrily at the posts, and then pulled strings taught, red in the face with stress and fury. "In the middle of the night, when we all think they're having their bo-peep, what are they up to? They're unhooking tennis nets and putting them up trees. They may think it's a Bushey Park, but I say it's a pain in the neck. And look at me round-the-houses and me daisy roots," he added indignantly, showing rips in his trousers and boots. "Ruined with tree-climbing! I tell you, I need a tiddly-wink. And if I'm not mistaken," he added, sniffing the air close to Mr Fox's face, "a certain headmaster has recently had the same idea. Been at the gay and frisky again, eh, sir? And look at the time! Before dinner! Tsk! Tsk!"

Mr Fox blushed. He didn't like the way the conversation was going. He put on a serious face and changed the subject.

"Tell me, Ron," he said, leaning on the tennis-net post thoughtfully. "Do you really think it's the kids? Er, godfers? There is a feeling here that these events might be, er, supernatural."

"Supernatural?" Ron roared with laughter. "Was that why you had the vicar round yesterday? Nah! Godfers. These happenings have godfers written all over them."

"Well, if your theory is correct, Ron," said Mr Fox cautiously, "do you have any idea who the culprits are? Quite frankly I am at the end of my tether over this whole matter. Mr Fritz seems to think it is something called a pollyghost. But I'm not so sure."

"Pollyghost?" said Ron, putting down his hammer and rubbing his chin. "Nah." Then a cunning smile spread over his face. "Culprits, did you say? Guilty parties? Hmm. Tell you what. I'll keep my minces open and see if I can get a butchers at some of their rooms. Don't worry, headmaster. You leave it wiv old Ron, here. I'll have found them culprits by tomorrow morning, don't you worry."

Mr Fox gave a sigh of relief. He patted the caretaker on the back. "Good man," he said. "I knew you'd have an answer. What would we do without you!"

As he walked back to the school, he didn't see the evil grin that crossed Ron Grunt's face.

Signor Ruzzi was giving Tom and Miles' class a lesson in musical harmony and trying to explain the difference between a major and a minor chord.

"Ze major chord, he is happy as Harry," he explained, thumping out a chord on the piano. "He laughs, he smiles, he jokes, everything is okey-dokey. No problema, he say.

"But ze minor chord –" and here he played a gloomy chord on the piano – "oh, he is meeserable! He wanna jump in ze lake. He cry, he sigha, oh, he eez sadda, sadda."

At the end of this, Signor Ruzzi looked as if he himself were about to burst into tears. His huge moustache drooped and his eyes were damp and watery. Sheila was looking extremely depressed.

"Each key, he have major and minor. He eez like people – sometimes he eez happy, sometimes he is sad. Sometimes he is…"

"Yawn, yawn," whispered Miles to Tom. "Why don't you get the Gameboy? We can play it without the sound and he won't notice."

"OK," said Tom. "I want to go to the loo anyway."

He put his hand up and was excused. He raced up to their room, but when he got there he was surprised to see the door open. He slowed down and peered inside. There, fumbling around in one of his drawers, was Ron Grunt.

Tom coughed and Ron whirled round guiltily.

"Oh, er, just mending your bulb," he said. "I was up my ladder when a screw fell on the floor and I thought it might have rolled in here…"

Tom could hardly believe his ears. Surely you didn't need screws to change light bulbs, he thought. And how a screw could leap up off the floor and get into a shut drawer he couldn't imagine. Unless it had been open to start with. Oh, well, it might have been.

"I'm just collecting something," he said, keeping a cautious eye on Ron as he looked for the Gameboy. "These accidents, er, happenings. They must keep you busy."

"It's accident prone, this school," said Ron,

climbing up the ladder. "I'm kept working day and night. Never get time to take Tyson – er, Lucy – for a walk."

As he reached up to change the bulb a horrible smell came from his sweaty armpits.

Tom rather longed to open the window, but he thought it might be rude. And he didn't feel like being rude to Ron Grunt. "You haven't seen my Gameboy, have you?" he asked.

Ron grunted. "Never seen no Gameboy," he muttered, wrestling with the bulb.

Tom looked suspiciously around. It was nowhere to be seen. And it had certainly been there this morning. His eyes wandered to Ron's tool bag. There, sticking out, was the Gameboy.

"Excuse me," he said politely, "but it seems to have dropped into your tool kit."

Ron looked furious. "Why, so it has!" he said. "That's odd. Wonder how it got there!"

"So do I," said Tom, taking it out. He felt emboldened by this discovery. "You're from Lanchester, aren't you?"

"I am," said Ron, finally screwing the light bulb in and collecting his bag.

"You never knew a guy called Lanchester Larry, did you?"

"Lanchester Larry!" Ron looked as if he would explode. "Never! Never in my life! But why –" and here he seized Tom by the lapels and thrust his face frighteningly into his – "do you ask?"

"Oh, nothing," said Tom, feeling terrified. "It was just, er, there was a notice in the town, about, er…"

Ron had drawn back his fist as if he'd been about to hit Tom in the face. But at the same time there was an almighty cracking sound and an enormous piece of plaster fell off the ceiling onto Ron's head.

"Ouch!" screamed Ron, clutching his head. "Gawd! No wonder your light went! The ceilings are all in need of repair! I'll be here for the rest of me life at this rate. Now you scarper back to your old Joanna lesson, stop rabbiting and let me get on with me work." He stared up at the ceiling as the plaster dust fell like rain on his face.

Tom hesitated. Before he left he quickly ran round the room picking up his alarm clock, Miles' special diving watch and anything else that seemed of any value, and raced back to the classroom.

"You were gonna longa time," said Signor Ruzzi, when Tom returned. "Ze class, when you gone, we all like zees…" and he played a minor chord. "But now you back, we are like zees…" he played a major chord. "We happy. We feel we are dancing on hair!"

Tom gave a weak smile. Then he whispered to Miles. "He's rootling around in our room, Miles. He was about to steal the Gameboy – but worse, he's prying into all our things. You

73

know, I think all this talk of poltergeists is complete rubbish. It's Ron Grunt who's responsible for the happenings. I don't know how, but somehow he's engineering these accidents himself, to keep himself here for as long as possible. He was mending our bulb and while he was doing it he fixed the ceiling to fall on top of him so he'd have another job to do!"

But all the time his mind was racing. What was Ron doing in their room? And if Ron really was the murderer, how could they flush him out?

CHAPTER
FOUR

"A Satanic ring!" Mr Fox could not believe his ears when Ron Grunt came to see him that evening and told him his conclusions. A poltergeist was hard enough to swallow. But a Satanic ring! "Surely not in our school!"

Ron Grunt leant back in his chair with a crafty smile playing round his mouth. His hair was sticking up as if he hadn't washed it for weeks and his face was the colour of dough. He linked his fingers together and then, realizing what they spelt, rearranged them so his hands read: "RTUOLB.E".

"The evidence speaks for itself," he said, shrugging his shoulders and nodding towards an array of objects on Mr Fox's desk.

Mr Fox leant forward and examined them. "A magic wand," he said, picking up the stick from Miles' conjuring set. *"Great Mysteries of the World,"* he added, looking at Tom's book from Smith's. "A silver bracelet," he added, picking up a bracelet of Susan's. "I have to say, this evidence seems a trifle thin. Are you absolutely sure?"

"Sure as eggs is eggs," said Ron, narrowing his eyes. "First, there's three of them. Three's a magic number, you know."

Mr Fox didn't, but he nodded his head sagely.

"Second, this paraphernalia – wand, book and bracelet – are absolute essentials in the old magic rituals. And third, I've seen 'em at it wiv me own minces. Yesterday night, as I was coming back from the old rubba – rubbadub, pub – at midnight, I was taking a ball of chalk in the Noah's Ark you got down the bottom of the lawn, and there they were, dressed all in black, dancing and chanting. It gave me quite a turn, I can tell you."

Mr Fox's eyes swivelled a bit, but he got the general idea. "You can swear to this?" he said, leaning back in his chair. "You actually saw it? With your own eyes? I mean, you saw the godfers with your own minces?"

"I most certainly did, Mr Fox," said Ron. "And that Tom, he was holding Germans – German bands, hands – with Miles and they was dancing round that bird – she's a real witch."

"Witch?" said Mr Fox. "Rich? Snitch? B...

Please, you don't refer to my pupils like that!"

"Nah," said Ron, creasing up. "Witch. Just plain witch. Shame on you, headmaster!"

Mr Fox blushed. "I see." He put his finger-tips together. "Well, I shall have to think seriously about what you've told me," he said. "But if you could swear to it, then I think that is evidence enough. Your own minces. Hmm. I shall write to their parents tonight. Thank you, Ron. You are invaluable."

"Think nothing of it, sir," said Ron, grinning. Then he reached over to Mr Fox's inkwell, picked out the little ceramic container, put it to his lips and drained the contents.

"Nothing like a gay and frisky, eh, headmaster?" he said, with a vile chuckle. "Good place to keep it, I say. Cheers!" And he left the room. Mr Fox felt extremely unnerved. That caretaker was getting far too familiar. And he knew far too much.

"It is a Satanic ring," Mr Fox explained to the incredulous teachers at a specially-assembled emergency meeting. He was sitting in his chair, looking very puffed-up and important. He was a decision maker, a Satanic-ring breaker. He was quite sorry that Mr Fritz wasn't yet back from London. He would be astounded at what Mr Fox had uncovered in his absence.

"Mr Fox," said Mr Carstairs, "I don't like to contradict you, but a Satanic ring? Miles and Tom and Susan?"

"Three witches," said Mr Fox in a quiet voice, putting a finger to his lips.

"Weetches!" exploded Signor Ruzzi from his chair. "Weetches onna broomsteecks?"

"I don't think they have broomsteecks," said Mr Roy. "I mean broomsticks. In fact I find it all very hard to believe."

"I have the evidence here," said Mr Fox. And with a flourish he produced, from a plastic bag, the book and the bracelet. "And if this isn't a magic wand," he added, flourishing Miles' conjuring stick, "my name's not Mr Fritz."

"It isn't," said Mrs Grain. "It's Mr Fox."

"Just testing. Well spotted," said Mr Fox, going red.

There was a tense silence. Miss Shepherd sat nervously on a hard-backed chair, twiddling her fingers. "But why don't we let facts speak for themselves?" continued Mr Fox. "I have written this afternoon to the parents of all the children concerned and I suspect that once these creatures of the night are removed from under the roof of Burlap Hall, everything will settle down."

"Creatures of the night!" said Mr Carstairs, getting up. "You can't call those kids creatures of the night, headmaster! They're just ordinary, well, kids."

"Interesting that there are three of them,"

said Mr Roy thoughtfully.

"Exactly!" said Mr Fox, leaning forward. "Three! A magical number! What more needs to be said?"

"That's surely not enough evidence!" exploded Mr Carstairs. "What on earth have you said to the parents, anyway?"

"Nothing about Satanic rings, of course," said Mr Fox hurriedly. "And I trust the story will go no further than these two walls."

"Four," said Mrs Grain. "Are you all right, headmaster? You realize you're accusing them of something really dreadful, something that hasn't occurred since the Middle Ages? I would hate to think you were carrying on a witch-hunt."

"I have of course been most discreet in my letters," said Mr Fox. "There is no question of a…"

"They'll all get together and go to the Press," said Mr Carstairs. "It'll be all over the papers."

"Ron has promised me he will see to it that nothing gets into the papers," said Mr Fox smugly. "He has contacts."

"Ron!" said Mr Carstairs. "This whole thing gets fishier and fishier! What's he got to do with all this?"

"Why, he has actually seen them performing their magical rites down in the Noah's Ark, I mean park, I mean the wood by the lawn. He saw them with his own minces on his way back from the rubba! I mean, er, he saw them with his own eyes on his way back from the pub. And he found the other paraphernalia in their rooms, as well."

"Meester Ron, he is a bad beret," said Signor Ruzzi, twiddling his moustache. "It would surprise me if he were not the needle in the haystack."

"We are straying from the point," said Miss Shepherd. "Speaking personally, as I always speak, from the bottom of my heart, I have to say that I would not trust Ron further than I could throw him."

Mr Fox could not help smiling at the idea of Miss Shepherd, her tiny figure strained at the elbows, trying to throw Ron anywhere.

But then he composed his face. "I am sorry not to get more support," he said. "I have to say that from your reaction I am starting to wonder if the infection hasn't spread. You have never been involved in witchcraft have you, Miss Shepherd?"

"Me? Never!" said Miss Shepherd.

"Nor I!" said Mr Roy. And everyone except Mr Carstairs joined in enthusiastic denials.

Mrs Grain, not liking the way the conversation was turning, coughed. "Let's leave it to Mr Fox to handle," she said. "Let's see what happens when these children go."

"And if everything stays the same?" said Mr

Carstairs defiantly. "Then what?"

"It won't," said Mr Fox. "I can assure you. As always I have my hand on the tiller and you can be sure to be guided by me. And now – perhaps you would all like a drink. I took the liberty of bringing along a bottle of wine because I thought we would all be in need of refreshment."

It was Asquith Minor who saw the letters to Susan's, Tom's and Miles' parents lying on the hall table waiting to be posted. He lifted one of the envelopes and held it to the light, but it was too thick to see through. He couldn't wait to tell the three friends and at the next break he burst into the common room and broke the news.

"But why should he be writing to my parents?" asked Susan, puzzled. "I've done nothing wrong. Maybe they haven't paid the bill. But I'm sure they have."

"Well, the letters are there, waiting to be posted. I held one of them up to the light, but I couldn't read what it said."

"Asquith Minor!" said Susan, shocked. But when she told Miles and Tom they were much more worried. It was the work of a moment for Tom to dart into the hall and sneak the letters into his pocket and soon Miles and Susan were craning over his shoulder in his room as he slit open the first envelope with a penknife.

He unfolded the letter and started to read:

Dear Mr and Mrs Sanders,

It is with great regret that I have to ask you to remove your daughter Susan from the school. Unfortunately, this term has been beset with strange happenings and unfortunate incidents too numerous to mention here. I have now received evidence that your daughter is one of the three ringleaders involved in the disruptive behaviour, and as it is affecting the daily running of our school I have no other option but to request her removal.

It is with great sadness and not without much thought that I and my staff have decided to take this distressing action. I would be glad to know of the earliest date you can remove her. I am sure you will appreciate my difficulties and take steps to collect her as soon as possible, preferably in the next few days.

Yours sincerely,

Mr Fox

"*What!*" said Susan, her red frizzy hair sticking out as if she'd been plugged into an electric socket in a cartoon strip. Her face was ashen. "Ringleader! Strange happenings! I can't leave Burlap Hall! Where would I go? It's the middle of term! I've got my exams!"

Tom and Miles looked shocked. "What on earth is Mr Fox on about?" said Tom.

"Poltergeists!" said Miles, snapping his fingers. "I bet Mr Fritz told Mr Fox about his poltergeist theory before he left to do his research and Mr Fox is expelling all the adolescent kids!"

"But if he were doing that," said Tom, pulling the other letters from his pocket, "he'd expel more than just us three, surely!"

Taking his penknife he recklessly eased it under the flaps on the other two envelopes, pulled out the letters and glanced at them. Sure enough, they all bore exactly the same message; only the names had been changed.

"Well," he said. "They're not going any further, that's for sure!" He stuffed them into the wastepaper basket.

"But won't Mr Fox wonder what's happened to them when none of the parents have received them?"

"Poltergeists," said Miles, grinning.

"Or Ron Grunt," said Tom. "You know, the more I think about it, the more convinced I am that Ron Grunt is behind all this. What's this evidence he's talking about anyway? I wonder if it's got anything to do with that *Great Mysteries* book disappearing."

"My conjuring stick's gone, too," said Miles, frowning.

"And so has my bracelet!" said Susan.

"But that means nothing," said Tom. "They're meaningless."

"Together they might look different. With some cock-and-bull story thrown in," said Miles. "Though I can't think what."

"It's Ron, I'm convinced of it," said Tom. "I'm certain that if we could just expose him and he were to leave, then all these happenings would stop. I just feel evil leaking out of him."

"But how can we expose him?" asked Miles.

"An anonymous letter to Mr Fox?" said Susan, sitting down on the bed and wrinkling her brow.

"That wouldn't do much good," said Tom. "He'd just throw it away."

"What we need is a huge piece of writing in the sky saying, 'Is Ron responsible for all the horrible happenings and did he murder Lanchester Larry?'" said Miles. "But that would be rather difficult to arrange."

Tom got up and stared out of the window. The lawn stretched in front of him, immaculate and green now Ron had taken to watering it and cutting it every few days. He looked down, and an idea came to him.

"Or a giant notice on the lawn, just under Mr Fox's window," he said.

"We'd be seen," said Miles.

"Not if we do it my way," said Tom, grinning. "I've got an idea! Why don't we write it in weedkiller? Then no one would notice it was us!"

Miles jumped up. "You mean put some in a bottle and then write it on the lawn and wait for the grass to die and show up the message? The following day?"

"Precisely," said Tom. "No one would know it was us because we'd just be hanging around the lawn with a bottle of something, and the message wouldn't appear till the day after!"

"We could ring the police instead..."

"Who'd believe us? An anonymous call from a school saying the caretaker was a murderer? No policeman in his right mind would take a call from us seriously. We're kids. They'd hear it in our voices. No, this way we'd really flush him out. And if he is the murderer, he'll pack his bags and leave and the school will be left in peace."

"And we could stay on," said Susan. "It's a great idea. Let's do it this evening, as soon as possible. If we can get these happenings to stop before Mr Fox realizes our parents haven't got the letters, then he won't write to them again, I'm sure."

They found the weedkiller in Ron's shed. The hut was in the middle of the vegetable garden, and the door was open.

"What are we looking for?" asked Susan,

sniffing the smell of creosote and compost.

"Weedkiller," said Tom impatiently. "Anything with Deadly Poison written on it, or anything called Weedo-Smite or Zappo-Weed or something like that."

Eventually they found a bottle of something that smelled absolutely horrible called Termino-Gro.

Diluting the stuff and finding a bottle big enough to pour it all into was difficult enough and it was just starting to get dark when they cautiously paced the lawn, writing their message.

They had considered: "Ron Grunt, your game is up!" but Susan said it was too vague. And "Ron Grunt is responsible for all the weird happenings and he's also Lanchester Larry's murderer" had been given the thumbs down because it was too long. They settled on "Did Ron Grunt kill Lanchester Larry?"

If there had been anything to see they would have surveyed their handiwork when they finished. But their work was invisible; there was nothing but an immaculate lawn, dark green in the fading light.

"That should put the wind up him," said Tom, as he carefully poured the rest of the weedkiller down a drain. "If that doesn't get rid of him and his stupid tricks, then I don't know what will!"

But as they slipped back into the school

Miles heard a noise behind them.

They stopped. "What was that?" said Susan fearfully.

"I don't know," said Tom. But he suddenly saw a shadow disappearing round a corner and there was a low growl that sounded as if it came from a dog.

They froze. "Ron!" said Miles. "Do you think he saw us?"

"If he did he won't have a clue what we were up to," said Tom in a voice far more confident than he felt. Suddenly he rather wished they hadn't done it. He looked back at the lawn. They couldn't undo what they had done. There was absolutely no sign of the weedkiller, and if they'd wanted to erase their message by chucking more weedkiller on, they wouldn't have known where to start.

Mr Fritz had made good progress at the Royal Institute of Poltergeists. It was a curious building in north London, half hidden by ivy and wistaria. He had been expecting it to be full of people flying into the air and chock-a-block with muddled files and upturned desks, but the whole set-up was a model of efficiency.

The hall was painted grey and black, with a gleaming stainless steel staircase rising to the upper floors. Behind a desk in the reception area sat a man in a grey suit with a sober tie.

"May I help you, sir?" he asked.

"Er, this *is* the Royal Institute of Poltergeists, isn't it?" said Mr Fritz nervously. It seemed more like a private hospital.

"It is indeed, sir," said the man. "This is where we log all reports of poltergeist happenings and try to get a demographic map of the occurrences. Combined with area profiles fed into our computers we hope, in the year 2010, to be able to give a much clearer idea of when and where poltergeists have struck and when and where they will be likely to strike again."

"Well, I think we have one at the school where I work," said Mr Fritz anxiously. "But we want to get rid of it."

The man's expression changed.

"Get rid of it!" he exclaimed. "Is that advisable? I feel it would be much more sensible to get to the bottom of it, investigate it, bring us your findings and take it from there."

"Impossible," said Mr Fritz. "We have no time. It's making life at school intolerable. If indeed it is a poltergeist."

"Describe it," said the man.

And after Mr Fritz had told him what exactly had been going on in the way of flying plates, errant pieces of chalk, slamming piano lids, exploding light bulbs, chairs slipped from under people's bottoms and so on, the man nodded thoughtfully.

"Certainly sounds like a poltergeist to me," he said. "But you realize that to get rid of it would be extremely difficult. And I'm not sure that we would go along with the idea of eliminating it anyway. There are moves afoot in the European Community to make poltergeists a protected species, you know."

"Protected species!" Mr Fritz's spectacles nearly flew off in indignation. "How can they be a protected species! There's even argument as to whether they really exist or not."

"Not here, there isn't," said the man, tapping some information into his computer. "I shall see when our top expert, Professor Flugelhorn, is free so you can consult him for advice."

He made an appointment for Mr Fritz the following day and the science teacher went back to his lodgings, happy that at last he was getting to the heart of the problem. It certainly was a relief, he thought, as he turned out the light, to know that in this room at least he could be sure of waking up and finding everything in the same place as it had been the night before.

When Mr Fox woke in the morning he had a slightly sick feeling in the pit of his large stomach. Today the parents would be getting his letters, and he couldn't say he looked forward to the furious calls from six mothers and fathers. It was the mothers who would be the worst – some women who seemed perfectly normal

when they came with their children to the
school would turn into screaming harridans
when you made any criticism of their off-
spring. But what was even more sinister was
that the phone was ominously silent – and he
wondered if they weren't all ganging up with
one another to present a united front. He
always made it a policy to allow parents to
meet as little as possible because alone they
were far less powerful than in maddened
groups – but their silence was strange, indeed.
He wondered, vaguely, if the pollyghost, or
whatever Mr Fritz had called it, had got to the
telephones. It certainly seemed to have got to
the grass, he noticed. Or was that the moles?
There were some funny brown bits on it that
almost looked like writing – the odd circle and
one bit that looked like a G, but nothing was
clear. Probably some beastly fungus – still, Ron
could handle that.

The caretaker certainly had had enough on
his hands recently. Each morning he had to go
round the school putting right what the
poltergeist had mucked about with during the
night. Lamps had been moved from one place
to another; test tubes had been smashed.
Signor Ruzzi reported that all the white keys
on his piano had turned black; Mrs Grain had
been sitting reading Latin grammar in a chair
in the common room when the chair had risen
from the ground, floated across the room, and

tipped her out the other side. There was the time when the loo lids had all been mysteriously glued to the seats which had been glued to the bowls, which left everyone hopping until Ron unstuck them; one afternoon after games all the boys' clothes had been swapped with the girls' in their various changing huts. One night all the taps in everyone's rooms had been turned on, causing a terrible flood. Another day Mr Roy woke to find that the cushions on his sofa had been stuffed into where the drawers had been in his chest-of-drawers – and all the drawers were arranged like cushions on his sofa. And mealtimes were a nightmare – with water being thrown, plates flying, and forks whizzing like arrows from one end of the dining room to the other.

The headmaster put a comb through the few hairs on his head and sighed. Life certainly wasn't easy.

That same morning, Mr Fritz woke in his lodgings full of optimism. He took a bus to the Institute and, at midday, was ushered into the presence of Professor Flugelhorn.

Professor Flugelhorn was so hairy and wild and woolly that he made Mr Fritz look like a suave executive by comparison. He had a bushy, grey beard and an enormous, heavy pair of glasses that seemed to be secured to his head by a thick elastic band. Mr Fritz noticed that his watch strap had been bound with plaster to his skin and, looking down, saw that his shoes seemed to be tied to his feet with string. He wore a belt *and* braces to keep up his trousers and on his hand, Mr Fritz spotted a piece of strong twine running from his signet ring up his sleeve, in rather the same way that little children sometimes have their gloves attached to each other through the arms of their coats.

They shook hands and Mr Fritz coughed as he sat down. He thought Professor Flugelhorn was a trifle peculiar.

"Forgive my attire, Mr Fritz," exclaimed the professor. "Because the poltergeists do not understand how much I care for them and fear any investigation into their existence, they wage a constant war against me. And that is why – " he gestured down at his clothes – "I have to dress in this way. Unless I secure all my clothes extremely tightly and firmly, a poltergeist will come and drag them off me."

"Drag them off you?" said Mr Fritz.

"Yes, indeed." Professor Flugelhorn shook his head. "Many is the time that my assistant has found me here completely naked, poltergeists having stripped off all my clothes, my shoes, my spectacles, my ring – everything. So you see, I have learnt by experience. I make it difficult for them. Oh, yes, they pull, they tug, but they don't succeed. So now, how can I help you?"

When Mr Fritz had explained the situation, Professor Flugelhorn looked serious. He put his fingers together.

"Perhaps first I had better explain exactly what a poltergeist is," he said. "The word derives from the German, literally meaning 'noise spirit'. But of course poltergeists are much more than noisy spirits. They have been known to indulge in fire-raising of a spontaneous nature, hurling objects, writing on walls and even scratching people. They can levitate people as well as objects and cause objects to disappear and re-materialize in another place. Sometimes they can cause liquids to spout up through floors or from ceilings.

"In the past if there was a woman in the house where a poltergeist appeared she would be burnt as a witch. Now of course we know better. And though many argue that poltergeists are merely a result of fraud and trickery, several cases have convinced us that however clever were the perpetrators of such fraud, they could never achieve the results that poltergeists are responsible for. Some say they are hallucinations on the part of the beholders. But when so many people witness the happenings, this seems unlikely."

Mr Fritz was starting to twiddle his thumbs here and look out of the window, rather like a pupil in one of his own science classes.

"There is the geophysical theory, which

explains the happenings in terms of soil mechanics and house construction stresses. But naturally we can discount this, as we can discount the psychoneurotic, mediumistic and Gestalt theories," he added, looking to Mr Fritz for support.

"Oh, indeed, indeed!" said Mr Fritz, laughing as if only a child would ever think of those as an answer. He had no idea what they meant, but he just hoped Professor Flugelhorn wouldn't take it into his head to explain them to him.

"So, having proved the existence of poltergeists, we now come to the actual poltergeists themselves. There are poltergeists and poltergeists, and here at the Institute we evaluate them on a range of one to ten. A poltergeist evaluated at one is a harmless enough creature. It may hide your socks and steal unfinished biscuits. But it is basically harmless. A poltergeist that rates a ten, however, is a menace. It can trip people up, cause quite serious accidents, family break-ups and even suicide. This is a poltergeist that has to be dealt with firmly."

"And where would you put our poltergeist, if indeed it is a poltergeist?" Mr Fritz was eager to get to the heart of the matter.

"I would rate it around nine," said Professor Flugelhorn. "From what you have told me."

"And what can we do about it?" asked Mr

Fritz desperately. "It is completely disrupting life at the school. Since I just happened to mention the connection between poltergeists and adolescent children, our headmaster is thinking of writing to the parents of all pupils around that age and asking them to leave! It is that serious!"

Professor Flugelhorn looked at Mr Fritz and roared with laughter. "Ask them to leave! That won't help! That is a ridiculous idea! Who put that old wives' tale into his head?"

"Er, um," said Mr Fritz. "Well, I – ah – had read somewhere that, ah…"

"Completely out of date, that way of thinking," said Professor Flugelhorn. "No, the current theory about poltergeists is that they are loose balls of old, unhappy spirits making trouble. We even have some evidence to prove this. Adolescent kids! Ha ha! Haven't heard that theory in quite a long time!"

Mr Fritz's heart sank. He just hoped Mr Fox was taking his advice and holding back from taking any action until he got back.

"But, Professor Flugelhorn," he said despairingly, "I hope you'll excuse me, but I haven't really come to London to hear about the theory of poltergeists or what grade ours is. What I really want to know is – how do we get rid of it? Our lives are intolerable!"

Professor Flugelhorn jumped up and started to pace the room. "This is the most extraordinary request," he said. "Most people who have poltergeists are fascinated by them. They are keen to let us research them. They are eager to sell their stories to television, to the Sunday tabloids. They are even interested in having films made about them." (Mr Fritz smiled to himself. He could just imagine Mr Fox and himself starring in *The Nightmare of Burlap Hall* or *School of Spooks*.) "But you – you want to get rid of yours. That is an extremely difficult question to answer. Or let me put it another way. It is an extremely easy question to answer, but an extremely difficult answer to put into practice."

"Why?" asked Mr Fritz.

"Because," said Professor Flugelhorn, "the only person I know of who can defuse a poltergeist lives in Brazil."

"Well?" said Mr Fritz. "Difficult, perhaps, to get the money to bring him over, but not impossible."

"Nearly," said Professor Flugelhorn. "You see he lives in the middle of the Amazon jungle and he is a witch-doctor – 120 years old!"

Mr Fritz's hopes were dashed.

"Address?" he said, not very hopefully.

Professor Flugelhorn shook his head. "No address. All I have is his name."

"Well, that would be better than nothing," said Mr Fritz. "What is it?"

Professor Flugelhorn rummaged in his

drawer. "I shall write it on a piece of paper," he said. "I suggest you keep very quiet about it. We never speak the man's name here – it drives poltergeists wild."

"Why, are they frightened?"

"We don't know," said Professor Flugelhorn. "Either they're frightened or excited. But the last time I mentioned his name we had trouble here for weeks. Our computer system was completely up the creek, filing system off the wall, and nearly all our office furniture was broken. So, please – be discreet."

He handed Mr Fritz a piece of paper, folded over.

Mr Fritz took it and opened it. "Aha," he said in a loud voice. "Papa Maracas! That's an interesting name!"

"My dear man," cried Professor Flugelhorn, putting his hands to his head. "Keep your voice down!" He jumped up from his desk. "Have you no sense in your head at all! Get out of here – as soon as you can!"

Mr Fritz gathered up his things and left, apologizing. Back in the professor's office came strange, twanging sounds of braces being pulled and tearing noises of sleeves being ripped off jackets, accompanied by groans from the professor. Mr Fritz hurried out of the building and went back to his lodgings.

The day that Mr Fritz was due to return was

the morning that the weedkiller worked. Tom and Miles had been up half the night in their dressing gowns, staring down at the lawn in front of them, and as the dawn started to break they slowly made out the letters written clearly in dead grass.

Did Ron Grunt kill Lanchester Larry?

"Oh, dear," said Tom. "I don't think we should have done this after all." But as he spoke, Miles put a hand over his mouth. "Look!" he said.

Round the corner, in the early dawn, came Ron. He walked to the beginning of the sentence, read it very slowly (it was much more difficult to read on the ground than from above) and then glanced up. Tom and Miles just managed to dive out of view before he spotted them. But peeping out from behind the curtains they saw him dash off towards his shed.

"What do you think he's doing?" said Tom. "Will we ever see him again? Has it worked?"

Miles pointed. In the distance he could see Ron, puffing and panting, pulling an old Rotavator behind him.

"Mr Fox will never see the message!" he said. "He's going to dig it up!"

Tom closed his eyes as Ron Grunt sparked the Rotavator into action and in seconds he destroyed the word "Did". Earth flew in all directions, clods of grass shot up, but the terrible racket brought a protest from Mr Fox, who flung open his window.

"Ron! It's six in the morning!" yelled Mr Fox. "Some of us have got to sleep! I've been up all night with my blankets dancing the foxtrot in front of me as it is! For heaven's sake, it's enough to drive a man crazy!"

But then Mr Fox suddenly fell silent. He had read the message. Although Ron was now whirling the word "kill" into a fine tilth, the words had sunk into the headmaster's consciousness. A terrible thought was planted in his brain. A thought that he immediately decided to ignore. It was far too dreadful to contemplate.

"Moles, headmaster!" cried Ron above the roar. And when he said the word "moles", a shiver went down Tom's and Miles' spines. He made it sound like spies rather than furry animals. "Moles in the grass!" he added, staring pointedly up at Tom and Miles' window. And again, the word "grass" seemed to take on a different meaning when it emerged from the lips of Ron Grunt.

"And by the way, headmaster," he added. "I've got something interesting to show you this morning." He put his hand in his pocket and waved three letters about. "Some letters I found in one of your pupil's wastepaper basket when emptying it! I think they were your own private property and I think they were stolen from you. And I think you'll agree that it's a very serious case indeed! When I've posted them for you, I'll come up and see you and we'll have a little chat."

At this, Tom and Miles sank to the floor. Miles reached over to the wastepaper basket. Empty. Obviously Ron had found the letters when removing the rubbish.

"We're for it, Miles," said Tom gloomily. "Now we'll all be expelled for sure. *And* by a murderer!"

CHAPTER FIVE

As Mr Fritz sat in the dark train, chuntering towards Lanchester, clutching a British Rail coffee and a "Bacon 'n' Bunburger", he stared rather gloomily at his reflection in the glass. He seemed to have confirmed his theory that the happenings were caused by a poltergeist. But, apart from that, he hadn't got very far. Why was the poltergeist there in the first place? How could they get rid of it? This Papa Maracas chap sounded elusive to say the least. What would he tell Mr Fox? He also wondered what the headmaster had got up to while he'd been away and just hoped that he hadn't done anything too silly.

Mr Fritz's mood wasn't improved by the sight of Ron Grunt, who had been sent to meet him, waiting in the school bus outside the station.

"Good trip, prof?" he asked, as he ground the gears into reverse in the station yard and headed off into the darkness to Burlap Hall.

"Hardly," said Mr Fritz, clutching his overnight bag as they screamed round darkened bends in the country lanes. "It's all very unsatisfactory. And I'm not a professor, Ron."

"Sorry, prof," said Ron. "There's been some odd goings-on up the 'all I can tell you. Oh, yeah."

"More, er, accidents?"

"As I see it, prof," said Ron, "there's three theories. It's poltergeists, what you was researching in London. It's me, tryin' to keep me job by causin' 'avoc, though search me why I should want to make work for myself. Or it's the latest theory."

"Latest theory? What's that?" Mr Fritz tensed up. Ron's headlights caught a frightened rabbit in the road and it only just scampered into a black hedge in time.

"Satanic ring," said Ron huskily. "And that's what my money's on, prof."

"What are you talking about, Ron?" said Mr Fritz. But Ron shook his head mysteriously and said no more, except, "I'm not sticking me bushel and peck out. I've got enough on me Germans as it is."

As they arrived at Burlap Hall there was an enormous crash. Ron peered through the darkness. "Chimney pot fell off," he said. "Gawd knows how I'll put that on again tomorrer. Sometimes I think I'd be better off in prison."

"In prison?" said Mr Fritz, startled.

"Preston," said Ron quickly. "Where me dear old mum lives."

It was two o'clock when Mr Fritz finally finished unpacking, climbed into his pyjamas and clambered into bed. As he did so, one of the legs fell off. He cursed. He reached for his glass of water. It flew into the air. Mr Fritz clutched his head in fury. Then there was a knocking at the door. No doubt that wretched poltergeist playing tricks again, he thought. He couldn't bear it. He put his head under his pillow and tried to ignore it. But it persisted. As he lifted his head angrily, he noticed the door opening a crack. He seized the glass that had finally come back to land on his bedside table and hurled it in the direction of the noise. There was a small scream and Tom, Miles and Susan came tumbling into the room.

Mr Fritz snapped on the light.

"What on earth are you doing here at this time of night?" he said, quite crossly for him. "I'm trying to get some rest!"

"We're very sorry, sir," said Tom. "But we couldn't sleep. Ron has got us into terrible trouble and Mr Fox has written to our parents asking them to take us away. There's a rumour that he thinks we're part of a Satanic ring!"

"So that's what Ron was talking about!" Mr Fritz rubbed his eyes as he got out of bed and pulled on his dressing gown. He lit his pipe and sat down in his armchair.

"Your conjuror's wand – your book from Smiths?"

"That's what Mr Carstairs told us. He was quite upset about it. He said we were all being expelled. What can we do?"

Wearily Mr Fritz decided to give up any ideas of sleep. And anyway, he wanted to tell someone of his experiences in London.

"So you see," he said, as he poured the tea. "I haven't really got very far."

Tom sighed. "Everything's such a muddle," he said. "I just know instinctively that Ron is involved with all this, somehow. I saw him prowling around in our room and I'm sure he stole those things from us and set us up. And as for the poltergeist, I know Ron can't make things fly, but it's too much of a coincidence, this poltergeist and Ron arriving at the same time. I just feel if we could get rid of Ron, the poltergeist would go. And if we could get rid of the poltergeist, Ron would go."

"And if the poltergeist went, there wouldn't be any more strange happenings and we could stay," said Miles.

"How can we find this witch-doctor?" asked Susan. "And what's his name?"

"I can't remember, I've got it written down

somewhere," said Mr Fritz. "I'll talk to Mr Fox about all this tomorrow and see if we can get anywhere. Certainly I'll see what I can do about the Satanic ring story. That's preposterous."

Mr Fox had no time to see Mr Fritz that morning. The reason was that his phone was ringing. And ringing. And ringing. Tom's mother was first on the phone. She threatened him with solicitors. Tom's father was next. He proposed to come down to Burlap Hall to "discuss the matter!" Mr Fox felt sick. There was a fax from Miles' father saying that unless he rescinded his decision, he was sending a copy of the headmaster's letter to the *Times Educational Supplement* (and Mr Fox suddenly wondered how many contacts Ron had there).

Later Susan's father phoned from the States and over the crackling line made it clear that he would be taking the matter up at the United Nations. In the meantime the only way to get rid of Susan would be to pay her air fare to New York.

"But that's impossible," said Mr Fox.

"Well, you keep her, then," said Susan's dad. "Simple as that."

Mr Fox sighed. "I'll buy her a ticket," he said. Secretly he thought that Susan was the ringleader and that if only she could be got rid of, the pollyghosting would stop. He summoned her into his office immediately after breakfast to get the whole business over with.

"Susan," he said, when she came into the room.

"Yes?" said Susan. The headmaster gestured for her to sit down.

"I think you probably know what I'm going to say," said Mr Fox, rustling through some papers on his desk.

"You're not sending me away?" said Susan anxiously.

"I certainly am. And I think you know why."

"I don't know why!" said Susan. "It's very unfair. I've done nothing wrong!"

Mr Fox looked up from his papers with a sly smile. "You needn't pretend with me, Susan," he said. "I know where all this trouble is coming from and you and your little coven of friends know as well, and frankly the sooner you're all got rid of the better, so Burlap Hall can get back to normal."

"Coven! But only witches have covens!"

"I think we understand each other, my dear." Mr Fox looked devilishly cunning. He felt like Sherlock Holmes at the peak of his powers. "We need say no more. Only that I have booked a flight to New York for you early tomorrow morning. So please – no more trouble till then, because your little game is over, I'm afraid."

Susan got up, her knees trembling. "You can't mean this, sir," she said, a mixture of fury and tears. "I'm in the middle of my exams, I've got all my friends here."

"Yes, your little 'circle' of friends," said Mr Fox knowingly. "Now, goodbye. I'm sure you'll grow out of this unpleasant phase you're going through and no doubt when we meet in later life we'll be the best of friends. But I'm afraid your practices are too disruptive at present to have you remain here. Goodbye."

Susan left the headmaster's study feeling drained and wretched, her head swimming.

On her way down the corridor she passed Ron Grunt, who was bending down repairing a banister that had flown off during the night.

"Hello, love," he said.

"Susan," said Susan disdainfully.

"You're looking a bit blue, penny for your thoughts, it may never happen."

Susan glared at him as she made her way upstairs to Tom and Miles' room.

"Oh, not speaking to me, eh?" He thrust his huge, scabby face between the banisters so that his mouth was at the same level as her knees. "Well, I think I know what's happened. Mr Fox has chucked you art. Try to abra-cadabra your way out of this one! Heh, heh, heh!" He chuckled in the most horrible way and went back to his pinning and varnishing.

Back in his study Mr Fox sighed with relief.

At least he had dealt with one of the culprits. Now there were just the other two to sort out. He looked at his watch. Eleven o'clock. Not too early, surely, for just one drink...? He pulled out his bottom drawer and took a quick nip from his whisky bottle. Feeling much revived, he noticed the latest copy of the *Lanchester Gazette* which was lying on his desk. Pulling it to him, he read: "Church makes £35 at village fete. New bypass planning application postponed." Very boring. Then something else caught his eye. "New clue in Lanchester Larry murder." He cast his eye over the story. "Police today announced a breakthrough in the murder of vagrant Lanchester Larry. They believe they may have found the murder weapon, together with the murderer's clothes, in a black bin-bag dumped on waste ground in a Lanchester backstreet. It was found by a..."

Anyone coming into the room would have thought Mr Fox had had a heart attack. His expression was the complete opposite to one of his famous "looks". His skin was grey, and his eyes, instead of starting angrily from his head, sank back into their sockets as if they had given up in despair. Even his ears seemed to have flattened themselves against his scalp in shock; what remained of his hair looked lank and defeated. The headmaster's blood had run cold. He remembered the black bin-bag. He remembered the low wall over which Ron had thrown it. Could it be the same? He would do anything not to believe it. But then he remembered that sinister message on the grass. Obviously the work of someone who knew the truth. Or, worse, perhaps Mr Fritz was right and it was a pollyghost. A pollyghost that had some very close connection with Ron Grunt.

The headmaster closed his eyes. He put his head in his hands. "Pessimissimus," he whispered to himself. Then he got up and went looking for Ron Grunt. The caretaker would have to go. There was no question about it.

"I've got an appointment with the headmaster at three," said Mr Fritz to Tom, Miles and Susan when they came to see how he was getting on. They found him in the science block between lessons, dressed in a long white coat and fiddling about with a bowl of liquid and some litmus paper. "I'll discuss the situation and hope that I can talk him out of this ridiculous idea of his. My problem, of course, is that I haven't much to offer as an alternative solution."

"Couldn't you go to Brazil and bring this witch-doctor back with you?"

"My dear, it would take money to get to Brazil, it would take me an age to find this character, and even then there's no promising that he'd either agree to return with me or, if he did, that he'd have any effect on the situation at all."

"I'm sure my dad could help track him down, as he's a diplomat," said Susan. "Give me his name, so if I do have to go back I can start searching for this guy – from the States." Mr Fritz scratched his head. "I've got it written down in my study. But I think it was something like, er, Father Drums."

"Doesn't sound very Brazilian, if you'll excuse me, sir," said Miles, who fancied himself as a bit of a traveller. "Wouldn't it be more likely to be Papa something?"

"Papa! That's right," said Mr Fritz excitedly. "Then there was a musical instrument – guitar? Kettle drums? It was something rhythmic."

"Papa Triangle? Papa Bongos?" suggested Tom.

"Nearly," said Mr Fritz, lifting himself up onto one of the lab tables and swinging his legs agitatedly. "Papa – Papa – something like macaroni. I know!" he said at last, beaming. "They were those things that Nick Stagger used to play!"

"Who's Nick Stagger?" asked Miles, baffled.

"He means Mick Jagger," said Susan. "Maracas!"

"Papa Maracas!" they all said in unison.

And as they said it there was a great flash; all the windows cracked, the tables collapsed and test tubes and Bunsen burners flew everywhere. Tom, Miles, Susan and Mr Fritz ducked as the poltergeist went into a great spasm of activity. Just as they put their heads up, another light bulb popped or another picture flew off the wall. Every time they moved, a table slid towards them or a chair rose into the air. It was a full five minutes before the chaos died down.

"What was all that about?" asked Miles, getting up nervously and dusting himself down.

"Phew!" said Susan. "That was quite scary."

Mr Fritz looked ashen-faced as he stared sadly at his broken dish. "Bang goes my experiment," he said. "But who cares? That was most irresponsible of me, I'm afraid. Professor Flugelhorn told me that if there was one word I mustn't say out loud it was Papa M—"

"Shhh!" cried Susan.

"Apparently that name drives poltergeists crazy. No one knows why."

"What's that smell?" said Miles suddenly, staring round.

"Probably my experiment," said Mr Fritz.

"No, Miles is right. There's a funny smell of – of old tramps," said Susan, closing her eyes and sniffing.

"Look, there's a can of Carlsberg Special on the ground," said Tom. Then he thought he shouldn't have mentioned it. Perhaps Mr Fritz was a secret drinker.

But Mr Fritz seemed very interested. "That wasn't here earlier," he said, picking it up. "It's very cold, too. Are you sure none of you brought it in?"

"Certainly not!" said Tom.

"Phew, *quel* whiff," said Miles. "Awful smell of, well, unwashed feet..."

"And unwashed hair."

"In fact," said Tom, everything suddenly falling into place, "I think I know who that poltergeist is!"

"Who?" said Mr Fritz eagerly.

"It's Lanchester Larry!"

There was stunned silence. Everyone felt their skin crawl. The very hairs on Mr Fritz's hairy suit seemed to rise.

"It *is* Lanchester Larry," said Mr Fritz. "I'd recognize that smell anywhere. But what is his connection to the poltergeist?" He scratched his head. "I'm going to ring Professor Flugelhorn," he said. "He's the only one who can unravel this mystery."

From a cupboard he produced a peculiar flat board of wood on which was assembled a small junction box, several different coloured wires, a little mouthpiece and something that looked like a plastic mug on the end of a piece of flex. From it ran a wire plugged into a socket in the wall.

Mr Fritz tapped out a few digits on a little metal disc on a spring, like someone tapping out the Morse code.

"That's surely not a telephone, is it?" said Miles.

Mr Fritz blushed and nodded. "Just something I rustled up during my spare time. I'd be grateful if you didn't say anything about it. I only use it in emergencies."

"But isn't it illegal?" said Susan, rather shocked.

Mr Fritz nodded guiltily. "But I only made it for fun – I've only used it twice... Is that the Royal Institute of Poltergeists? Professor Flugelhorn please."

After getting transferred to a Flugelhorn in Australia and then one in the Andes – the poltergeists at the Institute were clearly at work – Mr Fritz finally got through to the professor himself. He explained the situation and sat for what seemed to the three friends to be hours, going, "Hmm, mm... Not exactly ... but in this case ... yes, a murder victim, oh, I see... Hmmm... Hohohohoho! Rather! Any time," and all those irritating remarks that are so baffling to people listening to a one-sided conversation. He ended up by asking about Papa Maracas, but luckily Miles put a hand over his mouth before he could say "Maracas".

"Witch-doctor," he eventually blurted out, rather red in the face.

Finally he finished and shoved the contraption back in the cupboard. He looked radiant.

"Professor Flugelhorn says that the current thinking on poltergeists is that if someone has been murdered, their spirit may enter a warp in the afterlife and make trouble until it is released into the life-force of nature!"

"That would account for Lanchester Larry being here!" said Tom excitedly.

"We think Ron Grunt murdered Lanchester Larry," said Susan. "So that would explain why he's come to haunt him! He's been trying to tell us to do something!"

"Good heavens!" said Mr Fritz. "You mean Ron Grunt is a murderer?"

"Yes," said Miles. "But what about Papa – er, the witch-doctor?"

"Flugelhorn was a little bit more forthcoming, given the particular circumstances," said Mr Fritz. "He understood that in this case it would be a kindness to contact the witch-doctor. And he said he could be found somewhere in the northernmost rain forest, near a town called Galanga."

At this piece of information the Carlsberg can, which had been sitting on a table top, tumbled off rather disconcertingly and jerked on the ground before rolling under a chest of drawers. Clearly, Lanchester Larry had heard.

"Now I'll go straight to Mr Fox with this information and hope he can retract those stupid letters and somehow get me over to Brazil." Mr Fritz bustled off, leaving the friends looking anxiously round the lab. The idea that Lanchester Larry was there, with them, even if only in spirit, was extremely unnerving.

And, as if in answer to their thoughts, a glass cabinet on the wall, full of scientific equipment, crashed suddenly to the ground, leaving splinters of glass everywhere.

Mr Fritz couldn't have arrived to see the headmaster at a worse time. Having found Ron Grunt and got him into his office, Mr Fox had had to perform the difficult act of firing him.

Bright red and shaking with fear, the headmaster sat back trying to look cool and confident. In front of him, Ron Grunt stared back arrogantly, flexing his fingers by opening his hands and then making them into fists. For the first time Mr Fox realized what the letters on his knuckles meant. He gave an inner shudder.

"Now, I don't want to cause trouble," he said. "And I appreciate that you have been a great help here in the past few months. But certain information has come my way. About a certain, er, bin-bag. And I think it is my duty to inform the police."

The headmaster was particularly alarmed to

see Ron Grunt's face. He had hoped to reduce him to a quivering wreck. Instead, the care-taker simply stared back at him, his expression more and more unpleasant by the minute.

"However," said Mr Fox hastily. "You have worked very well here, and as a token of my appreciation I am prepared to tell the police tomorrow – to let you get away. But I cannot have you under this roof any longer."

Ron Grunt put his feet up on the desk and roared with laughter. "What! You read about this bin-bag in the linen?" he said, pulling the *Lanchester Gazette* towards him. "Oh, yeah." He chuckled. "Stupid of me, weren't it? I should have brought it here. No one would have found it here." He folded the paper and gave Mr Fox another sneering grin. "But as for goin' – no. I'm happy here. And here I'm going to stay until everything's died down. No one would think of looking for me in this godfor-saken place. And me and Tyson – well, we like it here."

"In that case," said Mr Fox rather grandly, reaching for the telephone, "you leave me no alternative but to ring the police this moment…"

"Oh, no," said Ron slyly. He pulled a wad of papers from his jacket and shoved them across the desk to Mr Fox. "Copies," he said. "Just copies."

Mr Fox put on his glasses and picked them

up. His heart sank for the second time that day. He didn't know how it was possible, since as far as he was aware it had never risen after the first sinking.

The documents were damning enough. Each sheet of paper was headed "Booze 'n' Binends"; they were Mr Fox's drink bills over the past year. Looking at the total it seemed to amount to hundreds of pounds. He would certainly not like anyone to know what vast quantities of alcohol he consumed each day from dawn to dusk. He knew he was just a man who could hold his liquor; others, he knew, would see it differently.

Then Ron handed over a list of the addresses of all the parents in the school – to show, presumably, that he knew where the copies of these documents could be sent if necessary.

"So you see, headmaster, I don't think you will be sacking me, do you?" he said with a curling lip. "And if any of your other staff have got any ideas, there are some quite interesting things I found out about them, too. Mr Carstairs and a married woman, Mrs Grain and her…"

Mr Fox put his hands over his ears. "I don't want to know!" he said pitifully. "Oh, pessimissimus, pessimissimus!"

Ron Grunt got up. He leant over the desk and leered at Mr Fox, his beery breath blasting out like poison gas. "You keep your north and south shut, and I'll keep mine the same," he said. "I'll nothing say about the pimple and blotch and the mother's ruin – and you keep quiet about anything you saw which you didn't. OK?"

Mr Fox nodded dismally. "If you say so," he said. He was caught in a terrible trap. There seemed to be no way out.

CHAPTER
SIX

Tom looked around the laboratory. It was getting boring waiting for Mr Fritz to return. Also, he didn't like the idea of being stuck with Lanchester Larry.

"The smell's terrible!" whispered Miles.

"Let's go out and look in Grunt's shed," said Tom, struck by an idea. "We can bunk off lunch. No one will notice. It's Grunt's lunchbreak and he always goes into his room to eat his sandwiches and beer. And I want to find what else he's got in his shed."

"Apart from what?"

"Apart from all that rubbish he's palming off as Satanic ritual stuff. You see, I wouldn't be surprised if he wasn't pinching stuff from everyone's rooms, even the teachers'. If we could find some stolen goods, surely that would be proof enough to get rid of him?"

"Are you sure it's safe?" said Susan rather worriedly.

"Of course it is. And there are three of us. He can hardly murder all of us at the same time, can he? And as we're going to be expelled anyway, we've nothing to lose."

Outside, the school grounds were wonderfully hot and silent – the particular silence that reigns during a lunch-hour. No bells rang, no tumbling steps rattled down stairways, no yells and shrieks came from the sports field. All that could be heard, far away, was the clatter of knives and forks and the burble of conversation as the entire school sat down for their meal. The smell of boiled fish mixed with the heady smell of wallflowers, and for the first time in ages Tom was aware of the birds singing. Usually he was too busy to listen, racing from one classroom to the next.

Edging their way round the lawn and through the wood, they came, finally, to the vegetable garden and Ron Grunt's shed.

"It's not locked," said Miles, seeing the door open a crack. "He can't have anything to hide."

"Nonsense," said Tom. "Of course he has. That's typical. Instead of running away to Spain after he commits a murder he lies low just under the police's noses. And instead of locking his shed, causing people to be suspicious, he leaves it open. Come on!"

Hearts beating, constantly glancing round for evidence of Grunt, they sneaked up to the shed. Tom opened the door, and they squeezed in. It was very dark and gloomy and smelt of a mixture of lager and lawn-cuttings. The shelves were lined with all the paraphernalia of a garden shed – oilcans, greenfly spray, fertilizer, weedkiller and so on. They looked around. Then Tom peered behind the lawn mower.

"There's a box file here!" he said. "Let's look!"

He pulled it out and through the light from a cracked windowpane they stared at the contents.

There were all Mr Fox's bills from Booze 'n' Binends. There were lots of letters of complaint from parents going back over the years. There, too, was a letter from Mr Carstairs to someone called Veronica, which started: "My darling, If only you were free from that wretch of a husband of yours, how happy we could be!" There, also, was Mrs Grain's birth certificate.

Miles stared at it. "Look! She's way past retiring age! You'd never think it!" Susan gaped. Then there was a letter from the Home Office to Signor Ruzzi about his immigration status, and a magazine called *Naturism Today* with a cover featuring a beach peopled by rather ugly-looking naked men and women.

On a yellow sticker and in Ron Grunt's ill-formed handwriting were the words: "Mr Roy". They were just wondering whether they should read the contents of an envelope addressed to Miss Shepherd when there was a rustling noise. It was followed by a rusty creaking and what sounded like a key being turned in a lock.

Tom started. "Miles!" he said. "What's that?"

Miles rushed to the door and rattled at it – but in vain. They were locked in. As they stood there, terrified, the shed darkened. Something had appeared at the window, blocking out the sunlight. And, looking closer, they made out the horrible, blotchy face of Ron Grunt, pressed up against the glass.

"Lookin' at my fings, eh?" he whispered hoarsely, through a crack. "Now you hand them to me through this 'ere winder and I'll let you art. Is that a deal?"

"It's a trick!" said Miles. "While we've got the stuff, we've got something over him!"

Tom looked at Susan. She nodded.

"No!" he said defiantly, glaring back at the caretaker. "We won't!"

Ron Grunt glowered.

"One more chance, I'll give you and then…" he gestured across his throat with the finger that had "T" tattooed on it.

"No," said Tom. But his voice sounded

rather squeakier than he would have liked.

"OK," said Ron Grunt. "You can't say I didn't give you a chance. Some would say it was a hot day today," he added cunningly. "But I'd say it was a bit nippy. Just the day for an Anna Maria. And as I don't think it's going to pleasure and pain and no one's goin' to be needin' their Auntie Ellas, I daresay I'll get a nice blaze up. See you soon, godfers!" And he disappeared from view.

"What's he going to do?" said Miles.

"Anna Maria?" said Miles. "Dire? Liar? Pleasure and pain? Sane? Rain?"

"Rain!" said Tom. "And Auntie Ellas are umbrellas!"

"And Anna Maria's a fire!" shrieked Susan, clutching onto Tom's arm as through the window she saw Ron Grunt coming back up towards them carrying a can. As he approached the shed, he sloshed liquid from the can round the dry wooden walls.

"Paraffin! He's going to burn us alive!" yelled Tom. "And then he's going to get off scot-free because he'll claim we were just fooling around with matches! We've got to get out of here!"

As he spoke, Ron Grunt reappeared so they could see him out of the window again. He put down the can.

"Goodbye, godfers," he said. "Oh, stupid old me, forgot me cuts and scratches!" He grinned foolishly and rummaged in his pockets. "Oh, no, tell a porkie. Here they are." He held up a box of matches so they could see them. "Sorry not to have known you longer!" He lit a match, threw it on the ground and all round the shed the grass blew up with an enormous whooshing explosion into a sheet of furious blue and red flame.

Back at Burlap Hall Mr Fritz was trying to talk to Mr Fox. But he wasn't getting very far. Mr Fox was in such a state he didn't know where to turn. He hadn't recovered from his meeting with Ron Grunt; all he knew was that he must go along with everything Grunt said or there'd be trouble. Stick to the old Satanic ring story, he felt. That's what Ron Grunt would want him to do, and what Ron Grunt wanted him to do, the headmaster would do. To the letter.

"But, headmaster, I have been to see the *experts*," said Mr Fritz, pacing round the room in exasperation. "All you have to do is hold your horses before doing anything with these pupils – and let me have a chance to go to Brazil and find this witch-doctor and bring him back, and then everything will be fine!"

"My dear Mr Fritz," said Mr Fox. "First of all I have good evidence of this Satanic ring and I am determined to get rid of the destructive influence these pupils are having, whether or not there is a pollyghost. The letters have gone off to the parents and Susan is leaving tomorrow morning for New York.

"Secondly, how do you propose to get to Brazil to find this man? Have you made yourself a pair of wings, pray? We certainly do not have the funds to, er, fund you to go off on a wild-goose chase.

"Thirdly, who on earth is this witch-doctor and how do you propose to find him? You don't even have his name. The whole thing sounds ridiculously vague. And as for the Royal Institute of Poltergeists, it sounds an extremely dubious establishment which I am sure is not recognized by any sound educational body in the world."

Mr Fritz faced the headmaster. He was angry, very angry.

"The evidence you have for this Satanic ring is total rubbish and you know it, consisting of a perfectly innocent children's book, a bracelet and a toy conjuring stick. It has been built up into a Satanic ring by that wretched caretaker you employed. I only wish I had gone down to the Job Centre instead of you, because, quite frankly, I am pretty convinced that this Ron Grunt is up to no good at all!"

Mr Fox went bright red. He hoped Ron Grunt hadn't shown Fritz any of the receipts from the wine merchants. He felt sick.

"Secondly," Mr Fritz continued, "I cannot believe my ears when you say you can't afford to send me to Brazil and back! You can afford to pay the air fare to New York of some wretched innocent pupil in the middle of her exams, but you can't afford to send me to Brazil to get to the bottom of this sorry business!

"And finally, once I get to Galanga in Brazil, I can assure you I will be able to find this witch-doctor. I have his name and he lives in the rain forest!"

His voice tailed off. It all sounded a bit weak.

"My dear Fritz, then let us send him a telegram and get him to come over here! There's no point in you going out and spending extra money!"

"You can't telegram a witch-doctor, headmaster," said Mr Fritz impatiently. Mr Fox had suspected this, which was why he had made the suggestion in the first place.

Mr Fritz stared round the room desperately. Was there no way he could convince the headmaster that what he was saying was true? Then he had an idea.

He leaned forward over the desk, putting his face close to the headmaster's.

"I'll prove it to you," he said.

"My dear man, if you can prove it to me, excellent."

"Very well," said Mr Fritz. "The name of the witch-doctor is … Papa Maracas!"

For a moment there was absolute quiet. And

then there was a low rumbling noise. Papers flew up from Mr Fox's desk and round the teachers like snowflakes. Mr Fox's chair hurled itself at a wall and smashed into a thousand pieces. The carpet suddenly rolled itself up from one corner, pulling all the furniture awry in its wake. The window broke, the pictures turned themselves upside down, drawers tipped out of desks and ink splattered everywhere. From the ceiling came the slow drip of a kind of treacly fluid.

Mr Fox crouched on the floor alongside Mr Fritz. "What's happening, man?" he said. "This is the worst pollyghost happening we've had yet! Make it stop!"

"I can't!" said Mr Fritz, holding his hands over his head to stop falling glass puncturing his scalp. "Only Papa Mar—"

"Don't say that name!" said Mr Fox sharply. "Things are bad enough."

"Look!" said Mr Fritz pointing. Because there on the opposite wall was a pen, poised to write. Slowly they read the words: "TAK MEE TO BRASIL BEFORE I TAK U!"

"The spelling!" gasped Mr Fox. "It's terrible!"

"What do you expect from Lanchester Larry?" said Mr Fritz.

"Lanchester Larry!" said Mr Fox fearfully. "Where does he fit into all this?"

"Our theory is that Ron Grunt is Lanchester

127

Larry's killer and that he's come here to hide out until the search dies down. But he hasn't counted on Lanchester Larry, who, being an unsettled spirit, has turned into a poltergeist to create trouble around him."

"My goodness!" cried Mr Fox. His brain felt even more confused than it was before.

"Now, headmaster, what is your response to Lanchester Larry's command?"

The storm appearing to be temporarily over, Mr Fox got up cautiously. "What does it mean – before I take you?"

"Heaven knows!" said Mr Fritz, getting up and brushing himself down. "Why don't you ask him?"

Mr Fox looked about him wildly. "OK, you take us!" He gave a wild chuckle. "I hardly think it's likely the pollyghost is going to take us to Brazil!"

But at that moment there was a rumbling and wrenching sound. The walls of the school started to shake. There was a crashing like thunder and Mr Fox and Mr Fritz felt as if they were in the middle of an enormous earthquake.

"What's happening?" shouted Mr Fox, holding on to Mr Fritz for support. "For God's sake, do something, before the whole school falls down!"

Back at the garden shed, the flames were licking the wooden sides. Miles and Tom put their shoulders to the door, but when it crashed open they were greeted by sheets of flame and black smoke.

"It's too late! We can't go out there! We'll die of fumes if nothing else!" gasped Miles as he tried to shut the door against the furnace.

But Susan pushed past him. "I'm going out!" she yelled. "It's only a couple of yards! It looks worse than it is!"

Pulling up her skirt and clasping it tightly round her so it wouldn't set light, she bolted through the door and straight into the fire. Tom had to shut his eyes at the sight.

"We've got to do the same," said Miles. "Otherwise we'll burn to death!" He took a deep breath and was just preparing to dash through the door when the garden shed started to rock violently. Try as they might to get through the door, they kept falling over as the shed twisted this way and that. Then there was a fearful crunching sound and Tom and Miles were thrown around as if a giant had picked up the shed and shaken it like a dice-cup.

Bruised and terrified, they crouched on the floor, their arms protectively over their heads. Then, as suddenly as it had begun, the movement stopped. Everything was still.

"Now!" said Miles. He flung open the door, which had slammed shut, and prepared to run when, just in time, he stopped himself.

"Look, Tom, look!" he yelled, staring down.

Tom looked. They were flying. Flying right above the countryside with fields and trees whistling under the shed's floor.

"Look, there's the fire!" shouted Tom, pointing down to a bright orange patch in the vegetable garden.

"And there's Susan!" yelled Miles. "She's safe!"

"But look, there's Ron Grunt!" said Tom.

"Where's the school?" said Miles, gaping as he looked down. Because where the school had once stood there was nothing but a huge bald patch of earth, outlining the building's foundations.

Tom looked down.

"It's gone!" he said. "But how did this happen? What's going on? Where are we going?"

Miles pointed out of the window. "There's the school!" he cried. And sure enough, straight ahead, the entire building, the whole of Burlap Hall, was sailing across the sky like a giant ship. The science block was floating along behind, and even the sports centre was airborne, though, probably because of the amount of water in the swimming pool, it was flying much lower than the rest of the buildings.

Slowly, but very, very smoothly, the whole convoy of buildings sailed right up above the clouds, like a magical city hanging in the blue sky.

"I know!" said Tom excitedly. "We're going to Brazil!"

CHAPTER SEVEN

The moment Mr Fox realized what was happening, he panicked. He looked out of the window at the clouds rolling by and moaned.

"Pessimissimus! Mr Fritz – this is terrible! We'll all be killed! And even if we're not, the parents will sue us! If only you'd never gone to see that professor!"

Because it was usually so red it was difficult for Mr Fox's face to go pale, but Mr Fritz was shocked to see that the headmaster's complexion had turned ashen.

"Don't panic! Don't panic!" he said in as calm a voice as possible. "Let me think!" He blinked wildly. "Call a meeting!" he cried finally. "Six brains will be better than one! And draw the blinds! Everywhere! Our passage is so smooth that unless they look out of the windows the pupils won't know we're moving.

You take the East Wing and I'll take the West! Get all the pupils into the dining room and lock the shutters so there can be no peeping!"

Blindly following his science master's orders, Mr Fox tumbled out of his office and, with a great deal of bluffing and bellowing, and conspiratorial coughing and winking at the teachers, he managed to herd the children into the dining room. He locked the shutters and put one of the dinner ladies in charge. Then he went back to his office, wiping his forehead as he went. He wasn't sure whether his best move would be to stop drinking altogether as his heart was obviously so bad, or reach immediately for the bottle. Since, he realized with a groan, there probably wouldn't be any bottles in the rain forest where they were heading, he decided on the latter.

The teachers were now assembled in the common room, each more bemused than the next.

"I looked out of the window and it seemed we were flying!" gasped Miss Shepherd. "Then Mr Fritz came and shut the curtains!"

"And ze greata rumbling. Eet is like a quake-earth," said Signor Ruzzi. "My piano I am frightened for."

"As far as I can see," said Mr Roy, consulting a compass, "we are heading south-west. Certainly the lines of latitude, er, I think, um, have changed considerably since earlier this afternoon. I was just in the middle of teaching Class 2a about the points of the compass and it was most confusing when everything went quite haywire!"

"Silence, silence!" said Mr Fox, standing up and clapping his hands. "I have an announcement to make." With that, he promptly sat down and turned to Mr Fritz, who looked back at him, rather muddled.

"Everything, headmaster?" he said.

Mr Fox nodded. "It's an unbelievable story, but I would rather it came from the horse's mouth," he said.

Slightly piqued at being compared to a horse, Mr Fritz unfolded his tale from beginning to end. This time he managed to refrain from mentioning the words "Papa Maracas".

"So," said Mr Carstairs when questions were invited. "We are expected to believe that this poltergeist, which is some kind of spiritual manifestation of Lanchester Larry, is taking the entire school to the South American rain forest at this very moment, in order to get help from some Brazilian witch-doctor." He was sitting astride a chair the wrong way round, his arms folded over the back. The position made him look extremely scathing, confident and sarcastic.

"Look for yourself," said Mr Fritz, gesturing to the curtained window.

Mrs Grain, who had sat silently near the

window throughout Mr Fritz's lecture, twitched the curtain with a supercilious smile. When she looked out she gave a small scream, then fell back in a faint. Miss Shepherd rushed to her aid. "It's true!" she said. "But we'll all be killed!"

"The floor won't stand up to it," said Mr Roy. "We'll drop like stones half-way across the Atlantic!"

"Now, now," said Mr Fritz. "Poltergeists have been known to cause havoc, but they have never yet been known to kill. There is no need to worry." He had no idea whether this was true or not, but, he reasoned, there was a chance they'd be safe, and if not there was no reason to die in a state of anxiety. "We have brought you here for this meeting," he continued, "to discuss what to do next. And, perhaps more important, since we seem to have no power over what to do next, what we should tell the pupils. Because if they or their parents find out we have flown to the South American jungle without getting any proper inoculations or, indeed, permission or passports, there will be all hell to pay."

"Inoculations!" cried Miss Shepherd. "If we don't die in the crash when we land, we'll die of malaria!"

"Or hepatitis! Cholera! Bilharzia!" said Mr Roy.

"Bill Harzia?" said Mr Fox, scratching his

head. "I don't recall a Bill Harzia at this school. I hope he's not here under false pretences."

"So, any ideas?" asked Mr Fritz, desperately trying to get the conversation back to the subject. He took off his coat. It was getting surprisingly hot.

"Keep the kids in the dining room all the time?" suggested Mrs Grain.

Mr Fox shook his head. "Not really workable. They're pretty much packed in like sardines as it is. And heaven knows what'll happen when one of them wants to use the toilet."

"And who knows how long we'll be in South America, anyway," said Miss Shepherd miserably. "We might be there for ever!"

"One thing at a time," said Mr Fritz, his heart beating with panic at the prospect.

"We can't tell them the truth, that's for sure," said Mr Carstairs. "A good lie is what we need."

Mr Roy was going slowly red. Mr Fox stared at him anxiously. Perhaps he'd caught cholera already, he thought. From the air. Or wasn't that possible? Or was it that the heat was getting to him? The school was going at one hell of a lick, certainly. It must be going faster than Concorde. Like Mr Fritz, he peeled off his coat and rolled up the sleeves of his shirt. Signor Ruzzi's moustache was covered with beads of sweat.

Mr Roy was now purple. And suddenly he shot up his hand.

"I've got an idea!" he said.

Everyone turned to him.

"Virtual reality!" he cried.

Mr Fox turned to Mr Fritz with his eyebrows raised. Definitely cholera – if not malaria – with a touch of jungle tummy thrown in, he wouldn't be surprised.

"When I was last in the States on a geographical workshop interactive information seminar," said Mr Roy, the words tumbling out of his mouth, "I remember someone mentioning that in the future, museums, with the aid of virtual reality, would be able to recreate entire geographical scenes – from long ago, from other countries and so on. So that pupils could go to the museum and actually experience what it was like to be, say, inside a volcano or in the Arctic waste, or on Mars. Couldn't we tell the pupils that this is what's going on? That it's not real? That though it may *seem* like the South American rain forest, in fact it's simply a virtual reality experience, laid on by the – the Lanchester Geographical Society?"

There was a stunned silence. Then there was a general murmuring of amazed admiration.

"Amazing!" said Mrs Grain.

"Brilliant!" said Miss Shepherd.

Mr Carstairs just shook his head and gave

the geography teacher a slap on the back that made him cough.

Signor Ruzzi clapped his hands. "You are a gene!" he enthused.

"Surely a collection of genes?" said Mr Fritz, frowning. Then, shaking his head and smiling, "Oh, a genius! Absolutely!"

"So we wait till we arrive," said Mr Carstairs. "Then we announce our big surprise and let them all out. Mr Roy can take charge of it all. It's a special geography project, eh?"

"And if anyone's seen anything out of the windows, then that was just part of the setting up," said Mrs Grain. "We can say the Society started organizing things a bit too early and was practising with simulated flight."

"Very good," said Mr Roy, nodding. "But I have to say I've never known the Lanchester Geographical Society being early with anything."

"That is the only catch in all of this," said Mr Fox, who had decided that they might not all be victims of dreadful diseases after all. "Virtual reality or whatever you call it I can just credit. The idea that this could be organized by the Lanchester Geographical Society stretches my imagination to impossible lengths."

"The kids aren't to know that, headmaster," said Mr Carstairs. "For all they know, the Lanchester Geographical Society is run by a bunch of yuppie whizz kids funded by giant drug companies and chemical organizations in the States."

Mr Roy had a brief vision of the society members he knew, white-haired or bald to a man, most of them in scruffy corduroy trousers and stained anoraks. He put it from his mind.

"I can see it all. I shall go and prepare the pupils right now," he said, getting up.

"That's the spirit!" said Mr Fritz. And the meeting broke up. Mr Fox and Mr Fritz went back to the headmaster's study, where even Mr Fritz accepted a large glass of Mr Fox's whisky.

"Bottoms up," said Mr Fox.

Mr Fritz winced. "Don't tempt fate," he said. "I want to land on my feet, please. By the way, you don't have a spare pair of shorts I could borrow, do you, headmaster? I haven't come prepared for this weather."

In the garden shed, Tom and Miles had worked out for themselves what had happened. By now they were hurtling over Mexico.

"We're going terribly low," said Miles, nervously. "I hope we don't hit anything."

"I wonder what on earth they're making of this at the school," said Tom. "It's getting dreadfully hot."

"I can't believe the speed we're going," said Miles. "Faster than any aeroplane."

"Talking of which, I hope we don't hit any

of them!" said Tom, peering out nervously. "I'm sure the flight controllers haven't bargained for this flight in their calculations."

Miles shook his head. Sweat was trickling down his face because of the heat. "I think old Lanchester Larry knows what he's doing," he said. "We're flying low enough that we don't need any pressure change to survive, and low enough to avoid other aircraft. But also high enough to avoid buildings and churches. Well, I hope we're high enough," he added, as they skimmed over the top of a grey cathedral tower in Caracas, Venezuela.

"I wonder if we'll be going via Guyana," said Miles, who knew more geography than Tom. "Or straight to Brazil. Hey, look!" he pointed.

Down below they could see a long silvery ribbon weaving through a jungle. "That must be the Amazon – or the Orinoco."

An enormous bird of prey suddenly passed by the window looking most surprised.

"Cripes!" said Miles. "I wouldn't like to be eaten by him!"

"Or them!" said Tom, pointing down. "I can see crocodiles! We must be getting lower!"

"We are!" said Miles. "Hang on tight, Tom. I think we're going to land, soon!"

The gardening shed circled round a few times and slowly descended. The atmosphere became hotter, steamier and more humid. Tom felt it pressing against his chest like cotton wool. The bottom of the shed brushed against the top of an enormous tree. Then, manoeuvering its way carefully down, it descended and shuddered to a halt in a small clearing in the middle of the jungle.

Tom and Miles stared at each other. What now? Their hearts were beating.

"Let's try to get to the school," said Tom. "It can't be far away." He cautiously opened the door and looked around. Knotted roots lay in tangled clumps around them. Parakeets squawked in the trees. Strange insects buzzed and chirruped in the dense, leafy undergrowth. It was quite dark down there, with only bright rays of sun piercing the undergrowth like searchlights.

Miles peered over his shoulder. "How do we find our way back if we get lost?" he said.

"The old Hansel and Gretel trick," said Tom. "Only not crumbs. Let's take the gardening string."

"Not long enough," said Miles. "Let's drop bits of paper."

"That file of Ron Grunt's," said Tom. "It's best to get rid of it, anyway."

They spent a few minutes ripping up all Ron Grunt's incriminating documents into tiny pieces, resisting the temptation to read them on the way, and stuffed them into a plastic bag. Then they set off into the undergrowth, scattering a path of litter in their wake.

It was the low throbbing of drums that led Tom and Miles to the witch-doctor's hut. They had hoped it was Form 2 practising percussion, but as they drew nearer they realized it was a sound unlike anything they had ever heard at Burlap Hall.

"Do you think we should go any further?" said Miles fearfully, stopping Tom in the undergrowth. "Perhaps they don't like strangers?"

"Nonsense," said Tom bravely. "Lanchester Larry wouldn't have led us into danger, I'm sure. He knows what he's doing."

"He never knew what he was doing when he was alive," said Miles. "So why should he now?"

Within minutes they found themselves in a clearing outside a grass hut – and standing in front of it was a witch-doctor. There was no mistaking him. If ever there was a witch-doctor, as his father would have put it, thought Tom, smiling to himself, this witch-doctor was that witch-doctor. He had very long, bony, brown legs with bare feet; round his hips was a small patterned loincloth, and hanging from his waist was a bead belt on which dangled an assortment of macabre items, like rabbits' feet, tiny skulls, bits of bone, oddly-carved stone. His bare chest was smeared with curious chalky signs in blue paint, his arms laden with bangles. And his face was old and brown and weather-beaten, framed by a circle of wild, white hair. His eyes were bright blue and piercing, and through his nose was stuck an enormous piece of bone. Tom wondered how he ever managed to blow it. This must be...

"Papa Maracas?" he enquired, putting out his hand.

And to his surprise Papa Maracas replied, "Tom – and Miles?"

"How on earth did you know?" said Miles, rather frightened.

The witch-doctor smiled. "I know all poltergeist hunters, all poltergeist news, everything in world of poltergeist," he said. His voice was hoarse and cracked as if he had been smoking a bonfire. From the ashy state of his face, Tom decided, it was quite possible, too.

"And Mr Fritz? He is with you, too?"

"Well, yes, but, er, heaven knows where or I'd show you the way to him," said Tom.

The witch-doctor nodded. "No problem," he said. "Your friend and mine, Lanchester Larry, will tell me where to find him. Now you both would like some refreshment?"

"Thanks," said Tom nervously, worrying that they were going to be offered some disgusting juice from a jungle pod.

But inside the witch-doctor's hut were rows of cans of Coca-Cola, a black and white television, a rusty fridge and a very old record player.

The witch-doctor handed them a can of Coke.

"Er, where is Lanchester Larry at the moment?" asked Tom nervously, after he'd gulped down half the drink and given the remainder to Miles. He looked round the hut.

The witch-doctor shook his head. "He cannot be seen – except sometimes as a ball of light. He has told me – " he tapped his head – "where he has put your school, and he will take us to it."

The school was only ten minutes' walk away, and they were helped by the sound of Asquith Minor's loud voice – that and a general jungle commotion that had set up around the arrival of the building. Birds flapped frantically in the trees, parrots squawked with horror, large birds of prey flapped busily to the scene, crouching on the upper branches to see if any food might be had from the occupants of the mysterious new addition to the jungle's scenery.

"Ugh! Gross!" Asquith Minor was saying as he inspected a squidgy-looking bug he'd found hanging on the bark of a tree. "Gosh, it even feels real!"

"Isn't this great?" he said as he saw Tom and Miles approaching. His jaw dropped when he saw Papa Maracas. "Who's this?" he said, putting out his hand. "That's really mellow! Why, he even feels real! Virtual reality's better than the real thing!"

"What do you mean?" said Tom and Miles.

"Weren't you there when Mr Roy explained?"

Sheila, who'd been listening to the conversation, interrupted and turned to Asquith Minor. "They believe they're *really* in the South American jungle!"

Asquith Minor roared with laughter.

"Aren't we?" said Miles, rubbing his eyes.

"No," said Sheila.

"Oh, you spoilt it," said Asquith Minor. "I was going to let them believe it. No, it's all done with mirrors, computers, holograms etc. I don't understand it. But it's all fake. Like your friend here." He gave Papa Maracas a poke and the witch-doctor looked extremely angry.

Miles turned to Tom with bulging eyes. Tom gave an uneasy smile. "Oh, how interesting," he said, rather unconvincingly. And they hurried on to the school.

"That's some mad idea Mr Fox has fed to everyone so they won't cause trouble with the parents," whispered Tom to Papa Maracas. The witch-doctor nodded wisely as if this kind of thing were always going on.

"But isn't it a bit dangerous?" said Miles to Tom. "I mean, they might catch something, or step on one of those beetles that get into your skin and then cross your eyeball every year."

"What beetles?" asked Tom worriedly, staring down at his shoes.

"Oh, nothing," said Miles hastily. "Probably only in Africa you get it. Still there are jaguars and tarantulas – no good thinking they're holograms."

At that very moment Mr Fritz came hurrying out of the front door of Burlap Hall towards them, wringing his hands.

"I've been looking for you everywhere!" he said. "I thought we'd left you in Lanchestershire! How did you get here?"

"In the garden shed, sir. Too difficult to explain now. But the problem is that Susan's left behind. With Ron Grunt! But let me introduce you. Mr Fritz – Papa Maracas!"

"Many welcomes to Galanga, Mr Fritz," said Papa Maracas, holding out his bony hand.

"And many welcomes to Burlap Hall," said Mr Fritz, grinning broadly as he seized the witch-doctor's hand and pumped it up and down. "Now, I hate to hurry you, but we must get the business here sorted out as quickly as possible so we can get back to Susan," he said. "I don't know exactly how we got here," he added, turning to Tom. "The whole school just took off to, presumably, the Brazilian jungle – that's where we are, isn't it?"

"Yes, indeed," said Papa Maracas.

"Let me take you to meet the headmaster, kind sir," said Mr Fritz, who was desperate to avoid mentioning the witch-doctor's name. "But, remember, speed is of the essence. Already the children are asking for water. We've got enough in the tanks, which seem to have come with us, to last a couple of days, but after that we'll run out – and no one will ever find us here!"

Meanwhile Mr Roy was trying in vain to control the school. He had called everyone in and organized a long class in the building itself, explaining about the South American rain forest, but everyone was dying to get out and have a look for themselves. Eventually he assembled them into groups and deputized the teachers to take them on a tour of the surroundings.

"But watch out," he urged, at the door. "Crocodiles may lurk in the river, there are many man-eating spiders, poisonous snakes and biting ants. Do not touch anything!"

As the tropical sun slanted in through the trees and the parrots and macaws squealed outside, all the pupils roared with laughter at Mr Roy's exhortations.

"Isn't it great?" said Asquith Minor. "He's really entering into the spirit of the whole thing. Even when he knows none of it's real."

"Well, if I were you I'd act as if it *were* real," advised Sheila anxiously. She had just got a very life-like bite from a huge green insect. "I wouldn't put it past that Lanchester Geographical Society to pop a real tarantula in here and there, just to add authenticity."

Asquith Minor looked worried for a moment and then laughed. He nudged Sheila. "Go on! You're joking! I'm going to go off on my own!" And he ran off to explore.

In the headmaster's study Mr Carstairs was trying to talk to Mr Fox. "No, headmaster, I *don't* think it's a good idea to open the window," he was saying. "It may be hot, but one of the first rules of the jungle is *not to open the windows*. There are all kinds of insects and creepy-crawlies outside that are just waiting to get in. Please bear with us for the moment."

"I shall die of heat," said Mr Fox, mopping his brow. He slapped an arm. "Ugh, these mosquitoes. Hope they don't carry orange fever."

"Yellow fever," said Mr Carstairs. "But I must be off to take the kids round the jungle." He was about to leave when there was a banging on the door. Mr Fox took out a comb and combed his few sweaty strands of hair over his bald patch, red with the heat, and rolled down his sleeves.

"I just hope it's that infernal witch-doctor,"

he whispered. "Come in!" he said.

Heaven knows what he was expecting, but he was not expecting a sight like Papa Maracas. True, he was hardly expecting a man in a suit, but he supposed he expected more of a doctor. Perhaps a man in a white coat. Even tribal robes.

"The, er, thing, er, man's not even wearing a tie!" he said, in an aside to Tom, who introduced them.

"He speaks English, sir," said Tom, going red.

"Speaks English?"

"I indeed do," said the witch-doctor, looking mightily peeved. Tom was terrified that he might try some of his magic on Mr Fox.

"Well, pleased to meet you," said Mr Fox. "Perhaps you'd like to sit down. No doubt you prefer the floor?"

"A chair is well OK by me," said the witch-doctor, sitting down stiffly.

"A drink?" asked Mr Fox. "Some, er, banana juice? I'm sure we could rustle something up. Or coconut milk? Or some water with a sprinkling of palm leaves on the top?"

Papa Maracas looked furious. "I would like a very large glass of the whisky which hiding you are in the bottom drawer of your desk," he said, rather sharply.

Mr Fox looked astonished. "Oh, I'm so sorry – I didn't realize that doctors, you know, their health, my weakness, of course ... how silly of me. As for hiding – oh, no. I just keep it there to stop the ants getting at it." He poured out a glass and handed it to Papa Maracas.

"Hmmph!" said the witch-doctor, after downing it in one. He turned to the boys. "I am not happy dealing with this old fool."

"Old fool!" Mr Fox's voice rose to a squeak. "How dare you call me an old fool!" But as he spoke an invisible hand lifted his tie high in the air, pulling him up out of his seat.

"Let go, you're strangling me!" screamed the headmaster.

"Lanchester Larry people to be rude to me no like," said Papa Maracas. "He knows here to help him I am. Now, this poltergeist, Larry, to be removed from your school you want, helped along his difficult path through the spirit world and into the forces of nature released, right am I?"

"Absolutely," said Mr Fritz. "He's been making our lives a misery."

"Of course. Between life and death is he trapped and his making trouble is cry for help," said the witch-doctor. He got up. "My equipment I have brought and the ceremony can I perform. I can tell from the signals that Lanchester Larry is giving me that he cannot wait into the natural forces in the jungle to be released where he will with the leaves of the trees, the wings of the birds, the shells of the snails, the scales of the alligator become one."

Papa Maracas had pushed back his chair and had set light to a small joss stick that he held in one hand. He started going round the room, half bent, with strange, jerky steps, his eyes shut, chanting in a curious language. The air became smoky.

Then suddenly Tom had an idea. He felt it would be terribly rude to speak, but this awful thought had hit him.

"Er, excuse me, I'm very sorry to interrupt."

"Silence, please!" said the witch-doctor, looking at him sternly as he continued chanting.

"But…"

"Buts no."

"What is it?" asked Mr Fritz in a whisper.

"Sir, if Lanchester Larry is going to be released into the jungle, how will we ever get back to Lanchestershire? And we've got Parents' Day in a couple of days, and not enough water. And anyway, we simply *must* get back, because of Susan!"

CHAPTER
EIGHT

At that very moment, back at Burlap Hall, Susan was sitting, shuddering with fear, hiding in the little wood that faced the school. She had no idea what had happened to Miles and Tom; the last she'd seen of them was when she'd turned back to see the garden shed surrounded by flames. Then a great gust of smoke had burst out of one of the windows and she could see no more. She had intended to run for help, but she knew Ron Grunt had seen her, so, her eyes stinging with the fumes, she had raced as far as she could away from the scene.

She knew Ron Grunt had seen her. She knew because she could hear him now, calling her.

"Susan? Susan? I know you're hiding in among the April showers and I'm going to get you. If you come out now you'll have nothing to worry about. But if you stay hidden – I can't account for myself!"

She could hear his footsteps crunching around in the woods and, worse, the scratching of Tyson's paws and the snuffle of his nose in the undergrowth as he followed her scent. She looked up. Perhaps she'd be safer if she climbed a tree? But it was too late to consider that now. If she moved so much as a fraction, Tyson's sharp ears would catch her and she would be done for. She longed to call out – but that would only alert Ron Grunt as much as attract help.

Grunt's footsteps got closer and closer. "Susan! Susan! I'm getting warmer!" he was saying in a soft, menacing voice. "Uncle Ronnie's coming to get you!"

If Tyson couldn't hear her heart beating, thought Susan, he should go to a school for the dog-deaf. She only had one chance. She took it – and made a break for it. She raced out of the wood like a rabbit, her legs pounding the ground. She tripped over a tree root, picked herself up and hurtled on. Ahead of her was the lawn. Beyond that was the school. Behind her, Tyson's footsteps turned to delighted bounds as he followed.

"Help me! Help me!" she cried as she got to the edge of the wood. But just as she was about to emerge she looked across the lawn to the school.

All that faced her was emptiness. Nothing.

Where was she? Had she taken a wrong turning? Susan felt as if she were in a nightmare. The scenery was all wrong. Where the school should be, it just wasn't. Or was she in a different part of the grounds she'd never been to before? Had terror made her lose her mind? Just as she was about to head across the lawn, across the empty patch where the school had been, her ankle was seized by toothy, slobbering jaws. Tyson had got her. She fell, face forward, to the ground.

Hard on Tyson's heels came Ron Grunt.

"Gotcha!" he gloated.

Half running, half falling, half being pushed, half being pulled, Susan was shunted through the wood, over the little stream that ran at the bottom, along the football pitch, keeping close to the sheltered side, and into a small piece of waste land where Ron Grunt kept his grass-clippings, compost, weeds and general debris. There was a tree at one side and to this Susan was led.

Roughly pushing her against it, Ron Grunt looked round for something with which to secure her. There was a piece of rope on the ground, and, tying one end tightly around her wrists, he took the rope round her body and bound her firmly to the tree.

Then he stood back and stared at her.

He looked particularly unpleasant. His face wore an evil grin and his tiny eyes sparkled with menace. Sweat sparkled in the under-growth of his unshaven chin.

"So," he said, staring at her. "What are we going to do with you now?"

Back in the jungle Mr Fox was getting extremely irritated with the proceedings. They had moved out of the study to get cool, but outside was almost hotter than indoors.

"Look, can't we get on with this?" he said. His face was scarlet from the humid atmo-sphere, and he felt there were spiders tickling him all over. He could hear the whoops and screams of his pupils as they explored the sur-rounding jungle with the teachers. He could hear Mrs Grain: "Don't touch that spider, Sandra!" Then Mr Carstairs: "They may not be real, Sheila, but we have to obey the laws of the jungle to enter into the spirit of the thing." Hard by, he heard Mr Roy screaming: "Help!" – but luckily a later furious expletive from the geography master reassured him that every-thing was all right. Foolish man. He had prob-ably fallen into a swamp. If he came out covered with tropical leeches, then serve him right. As soon as the school got away from this beastly place, the better. Before all the pupils went down with orange, yellow or even scarlet fever or, worse, were eaten by crocodiles.

"Susan's fine," he added angrily to Tom. "I saw her only a second ago."

"You didn't, sir," said Tom, flushing with anger. "Did he, Mr Fritz? She's back at Burlap Hall. I mean, back at whatever's there now."

Mr Fritz nodded anxiously. "Tom's got a point, headmaster," he said. He sat down on a knotted piece of root. Strange green plants dangled down from above on to his head. It was all so difficult. He stared up at the school building, which seemed dwarfed by the jungle. A large parrot was perched on one of its gothic gables. A snake rested on the windowsill of Mr Fox's study, its tail hanging down as if it didn't have a care in the world.

Papa Maracas tapped the bone in his nose angrily.

"Do you me my magical rites to perform, or not?" he said. "Working for you for nothing, I am," he added, rather crossly. "Where your school is, or what happens to this Susan is my business none of. In the business of releasing unhappy spirits – poltergeists – back into their natural environment, I am. Please let me on with things to get."

"I know!" cried Tom, who had been thinking. "Why don't we get Lanchester Larry to take the whole school back – including you, Papa Maracas – and then you can do your spell there! I'm sure Lanchester Larry would prefer to be released into his own natural environment, anyway," he added. "I'm not sure he'd really like the jungle if he's used to

156

the English climate."

The words "English climate" made the witch-doctor shudder. "Come to England I cannot!" he protested. "Your English fogs and your frozen winters I hear of. Of cold I would die!"

"Well, we're dying of heat!" exploded Mr Fox.

Mr Fritz put a hand on his arm. "The thing is, headmaster, that our kind friend here – " and he gave an ingratiating smile to Papa Maracas – "has something to offer us, and we have nothing to offer him. So it is not appropriate to argue about who is suffering most from which climate."

"You've lost me there," said Mr Fox. "All I know is that we've got to get back to England as soon as possible. After all – Parents' Day! My goodness! It's tomorrow! Oh, pessimissimus, pessimissimus!"

"And if to England I come," continued the witch-doctor, "how to get home am I able?"

This was a promising breakthrough in the talks. Mr Fritz leapt in. "We would pay your fare back, of course," he said. "And any expenses you might incur…"

"Rubbish," said Mr Fox. "If he's so bloody clever he can cast a spell to get himself back!"

"Please, Mr Fox, language, language," said Mr Fritz, wishing with all his heart that Mr Fox would just go inside and sit in his study.

Tom butted in. "I've got it! Larry takes us all back right now. Then Mr Fox can exchange the single ticket he bought for Susan to return to New York for a ticket back to Brazilia, and he won't have to pay much more and everyone will be happy."

"Done!" cried Mr Fritz, putting his foot firmly on Mr Fox's to distract him.

"Ouch!" cried the headmaster. "I've been bitten by a snake! I'm dying!"

"Nonsense!" said Mr Fritz. "You go and round up the teachers and get all the pupils back into the school. Tom, Miles and I will work out the final details with Papa Maracas. Because I am sure there are some things you would like from England that you would accept as gifts, no?"

"Like a new colour television?" suggested Tom. "Or a brand new fridge?" The irritation started to fade from Papa Maracas' eyes. "A seedy record player?" he asked, eagerly.

"You've got a seedy record player already," said Tom. "Rather too seedy if you ask me. What you need is a CD player."

"Exactly," said Papa Maracas, his eyes gleaming. "A few seedies by Queen, Michael Jackson and a little-known British group called the Inedible Stumps, and anything you want I'll do."

And with that he marched into the school, headed straight for Mr Fox's study and, pointing to the bottom left-hand drawer of Mr Fox's desk, demanded a drink.

It had been extremely hard work getting every pupil back into the school. Sheila had been bitten by something horrible with green wavy things coming out of its head; Signor Ruzzi had nearly had his best piano-playing hand bitten off by a slimy, hairy creature that had popped out at him from a plant as he was telling all his group to hush up and listen to the "museec of the jungle!" Asquith Minor had found a large snake twisting itself round his legs, which Mr Carstairs had beaten off with a stick. "Are you sure these things aren't real, sir?" he had asked, finally suspicious. "They seem awfully real."

"It's amazing what technology can do," said Mr Carstairs, who himself was wriggling and itching with what he was convinced were poisonous weevils that had clambered down his shirt.

Sandra had had to be persuaded not to bring back a bunch of wild tropical flowers she had gathered. Mr Roy could see several horrible insects lurking at the bottom of their enticing flower heads. "There is no point, Sandra," he said, as he snatched them out of her hand and threw them as far as he could. "They will only disappear when the Lanchester Geographical Society turn off their virtual reality equipment."

"But how do they do the smell?" Sandra had asked tearfully.

Mr Roy smiled knowingly. "Ah, that's their little secret. Now, into the dining room with you."

Eventually everyone was rounded up in the shuttered dining room. Asquith Minor demanded to go to the loo. Mrs Grain refused permission. "No, the way that the Lanchester Geographical Society dismantle their equipment is entirely secret. If there is any chance of your looking out of the windows they will never give you such an experience again," she explained, rather weakly. "You will just have to hold out, Asquith Minor."

And as she spoke there was a great rumbling noise, the school started to shake, the walls rattled, all the pupils hung on to one another, until there was a strange calm as the school slowly and evenly flew straight up in the air. Over the jungle, over Venezuela and straight across the Atlantic Ocean, smooth as butter.

"Amazing," said the witch-doctor as he peered out of Mr Fox's window. Tom, Miles and Mr Fritz all crowded round. This time they were able to enjoy the journey back. They started to feel better. Mr Fox unrolled his shirt sleeves. Mr Fritz put his jacket back on.

And Papa Maracas started to shiver uncontrollably.

*　　　*　　　*

Back in the grounds of Burlap Hall – or rather, where Burlap Hall used to be – Susan was terrified. Her wrists hurt, she could hardly breathe, and the more Ron Grunt paced up and down, trying to work out his tactics, the more scared she became. She could hear him muttering under his breath. "Hangin'? No rope. Wiv me bare hands? Not my style, though. Fire?" He shook his head. "The old Anna Maria didn't work last time." Then he snapped his fingers and his face broke into a smile.

"Stabbin'! Stabbin' it'll have to be! I'm a knife man meself and as my old man always used to say, stick to what you know best. Don't mess with new ideas, particularly in times of emergency. So it's off to the kitchens with you, my lad, and back here and finish her off."

Susan's heart had practically stopped beating; she didn't know why he didn't forget about the knives or the burning and simply scare her to death. Heaven knows it would be easy enough, she was half dead already with terror – but despite her fear, she couldn't help feeling relieved when he walked away. Maybe she'd be able to wriggle free and escape... Then she saw him stop. The dog, who was trailing after him, looked up questioningly. Following its master's order, it trotted back to the tree and, sitting down with its fangs bared, stared up at her, keeping evil guard.

Maybe someone at the school would wonder what Ron Grunt was doing in the kitchens with a knife. Maybe by now they'd realize that three pupils were missing and organize a search party? But then she remembered – that weird piece of landscape when she emerged from the wood; the barren field where the school should have been. It was as if – well, it was as if the whole school had simply vanished.

Meanwhile Ron Grunt had wandered back to the school, determined to slip in through the kitchen window and nick one of the carving knives from a drawer. It would be perfectly simple. He'd kill Susan, put her body in the shallow grave, and return the knife. When they asked about the three children it would be assumed that she was just one of the three who had got burned. He would have to check on that hut, now he thought about it. The shed had seemed to go up at the most astonishing rate, and a huge chunk of it seemed to fly into the air as far as he could see, but then he'd spotted Susan and his attention had been distracted. He just hoped those two boys hadn't got away – but there was no chance, no chance at all. No one could have survived that fire.

He was thinking all these things as he made his way to the school. When he arrived at the bare field where the school had once stood, he was gobsmacked. He couldn't believe his own minces. His jaw dropped, and he blinked. Then he pinched himself on the naked lady's thigh to make sure he wasn't dreaming. Then he pinched himself on the dragon's tail to make even more certain.

"What the...?" was about all he could get out. "What the...?"

Never mind. It was probably some freak of the weather, a mirage. The stress was getting to him. He shook his head. He'd have to take his bicycle, which he always kept locked up in a secret place in the woods in case he needed a sudden getaway, and risk nipping into Lanchester to buy a knife. The shops were still open, and no one would recognize him without his dog, particularly if he kept his tattoos firmly under wraps.

It was a rather dark and gloomy afternoon when the school returned. It looked as if a storm cloud was gathering. The sky was that particular greenish colour it goes, as Miles tastefully put it, when it wants to be sick. As the building shuddered to a halt Mr Fox let out a huge cheer. Mr Fritz rushed to the dining room to let everyone out (including Asquith Minor, who thought he was going to die from crossing his legs for the last half hour) and, apart from the presence of the shivering witchdoctor, everything was back to normal.

"You can borrow one of my jackets and a pair of jeans," said Mr Carstairs. "Can't have

you being cold, old chap." He led the Papa
Maracas up to his room and let him choose.
Unfortunately the witch-doctor took a fancy
to a particularly garish maroon-and-yellow-
striped jacket and a weird pair of old flares that
Mr Carstairs had kept from his rave-up days in
the Sixties. He also borrowed a pair of black
woollen gloves. But refused socks and shoes.
He looked odd, to say the least.

The dinner ladies managed to rustle up an
early supper that combined with tea, while
Tom and Miles rushed about the grounds
searching for Susan.

There was no sign of her by the shed –
which, despite being slightly singed at the
edges, had landed unscathed. The scorched
earth around it, caused by the fire, made Tom
and Miles shiver as they realized what a
narrow escape they had had.

"She went this way," said Tom, pointing
towards the wood. "I saw her from the shed
when it was flying."

They plunged into the woods until Tom
decided they might be destroying clues.

"The police wouldn't do this," he said.
"Remember the thin blue line."

"What thin blue line?" said Miles.

"When they're looking for clues. They make
a thin blue line and go on their hands and knees
looking for torn pieces of fabric attached to
branches and things."

"If you think I'm going to go through the woods like this," said Miles, dropping to his knees, "as if I were praying, you're mistaken. Hey – what's this?" Caught on a branch was a piece of Susan's skirt.

"See?" said Tom triumphantly. "On we go."

They found the spot where she'd been hiding; they found the tracks of Tyson's paw marks, and even worked out that Ron Grunt must have dragged her away – but where to? Once Ron Grunt had got her on her feet and out of the wood there were no tracks to follow, and call as they might there was no response.

"This is terrible," said Miles. "He might have murdered her! We must go and get help!"

Running as fast as they could, they rushed back to the school.

"The witch-doctor, he'll help!" cried Tom as they burst into Mr Fox's office. And there he was, being watched by Mr Fritz and Mr Fox, as he performed his poltergeist-liberating spell.

The desk had been pushed back and Papa Maracas had put his little totems on the floor in the middle of the carpet. Dancing round and round, in his striped blazer, with the bone through his nose, he was hopping with his special steps and chanting his weird verses as he went.

Not again! Tom looked at Miles, who was speechless.

"Er, sir," he whispered to Mr Fritz – but Mr

Fritz looked at him furiously. "Sir?" he said, looking at Mr Fox.

"OUT!" mouthed Mr Fox.

"Please," said Tom, a bit louder, on the verge of tears.

The witch-doctor stopped.

"It I will not have!" he said. "This is the second time I've been interrupted! This poltergeist to go away you want or not? Each time this spell on the poltergeist I begin my powers over it get weaker and weaker. A sensible boy who liked the Inedible Stumps I thought you were, but now just a stupid schoolboy who can't keep his nose out of anything I find you are!"

"Oh, sir, sir," said Tom, everything coming out in a rush. "We came in the shed because we were there with Susan when the school took off, we were spying on Ron Grunt, and we just found some horrible papers he seemed to have stolen…"

Mr Fox went bright red at this point. "That's enough, Tom. Ten hundred detentions!"

"But we destroyed them all," said Miles, butting in, "all of them!"

Mr Fox's face lit up. "When I said ten hundred detentions I meant ten hundred, er, lettings off from ten hundred detentions, plus the school prize for bravery!"

"And Ron Grunt found us and lit this fire round us and Susan rushed out and that was when the shed took off and we followed you to South America and left Susan behind and Ron Grunt's got her and he's either killed her or is about to kill her..."

He looked round the room desperately. No one seemed quite to understand what he was saying, it had all come out so confused. He turned to the witch-doctor, desperately. "Can't you do something? Or can't Lanchester Larry do something? He spent enough time frightening the daylights out of all of us at the school – why did he never tackle Ron Grunt, his murderer?"

The witch-doctor shook his head. "Impossible it is for poltergeist to attack attacker. But one last wish granted before unhappy spirit into atmosphere released. Ask him!"

"Oh, Lanchester Larry!" said Tom, begging into the air. "I did once give you ten pence! You must want to have your murderer brought to justice! You'd feel much better being released into the spiritual world if you knew you'd done a last good deed before you went! Lanchester Larry, please, please help us find Ron Grunt and Susan!"

There was a blinding flash, a terrible smell of old socks and stale lager, and a picture fell off the wall. It wasn't too late! Lanchester Larry had heard him!

At the tree Susan had given up hope. She had

heard Tom and Miles calling for her and initially her heart had leapt for joy. But however much she tried to scream, nothing would come out of her mouth except a burbling noise muffled by Ron Grunt's disgusting old hanky. Her throat ached with roaring against the handkerchief; her body was bruised with pulling against her bonds; her wrists were starting to bleed as she rubbed them together, trying to free herself. Even Tyson didn't frighten her now. The worst he could do would be to bite her. If she tried to escape, there was a chance that she'd be severely mauled but at least she'd be alive.

But the voices had stopped calling. Tom and Miles had obviously given up. She imagined them, back at Burlap Hall – if Burlap Hall had returned or indeed if it had ever been away – worriedly discussing her and thinking she would return later. She imagined her mum and dad and her brother and her bedroom at home, and she started to cry softly and despairingly. Then she saw a figure approaching. She looked up excitedly. Had they found her at last?

No. Walking towards her, a brand new knife glistening in his hand, was the menacing figure of Ron Grunt.

"At last," he said, holding the knife high, "it's time for us to say ta-ta!"

CHAPTER NINE

In Mr Fox's study, a whirlwind had begun. It blew all the papers from his desk, it whipped the central light round like an egg-beater, it sucked Mr Fox's remaining hairs away from their usual plastered place over his bald patch until they waved high in the air. Then it took off. Out of the door, down the corridor, and whizzing through the great front entrance, across the lawn, through the wood and on and on.

"Quick!" Tom had shouted when it started. And to Mr Fritz he yelled, "Get the police!" And then he and Miles, running for all they were worth, followed the long grey column of wind beyond the wood, past the football pitch and eventually to the small piece of waste land where Susan was kept prisoner.

"There she is!" shouted Tom, pointing. As

Tom spoke, Ron Grunt turned sharply, knife in hand, only to be met by the full force of the poltergeist whirlwind. It seized the caretaker in its blast; it picked him up and shook him around until his bulging eyes were popping out of his head. The knife dropped to the ground and Miles seized it.

"You murdered Lanchester Larry, didn't you?" he cried. "And now we're going to get the police and you're going to prison for a very long time!"

Ron Grunt tried to nod, but the poltergeist had suspended him in mid-air. His feet were a metre off the ground. And since, at the same time, he was being shaken like a rag doll, it was difficult for him to make any response. Finally Larry had had enough. The wind subsided and Ron Grunt was dropped in a dishevelled heap on the ground. Tom and Miles immediately jumped on his back and pinned him down.

Far away a siren wailed and within minutes four policemen were leaping from a car that had squealed over the lawn and ground to a halt nearby.

"That's him! Ron Grunt!" shouted one, getting out a pair of handcuffs. He came over to Grunt's wriggling body and said, "I am arresting you for the murder of a vagrant known as Lanchester Larry and would like to warn you that anything you say will be taken down in evidence." With that, he snapped the cuffs on the caretaker, and the other three policemen bundled him into the back of the car. Ron Grunt looked dazed and baffled as he was driven off. "We'll be back to take notes," said one of the policemen. "We may need you as evidence."

Peering through the window Ron Grunt gave a last look at his dog. "Ta-ta, Tyson, old son!" he said dolefully. And then, "Ta-ta, god-fers!"

"We'll look after Tyson," said Tom, who suddenly felt a bit sorry now he saw the care-taker trapped and on his way to a life in prison.

Miles was untying Susan, who was com-ing to.

"Miles! Tom!" she said, gasping with relief. "How did you find me? I thought you'd never come. And where's – where's…"

"He's been arrested, don't worry," said Tom, putting his arm round her. "He'll be locked away for a very long time. Now come on back to the school and we'll go up to our room and have a nice glass of Coke and I'll bring you up some tea and we'll tell you what happened and you can tell us."

"What's that dog still doing here?" asked Susan nervously, as she rubbed her wrists.

"We'll get the RSPCA to take care of him and he'll find a nice owner," said Miles. "It's not his fault he had Ron Grunt as a master. Is it, Tyson?" Tyson whimpered a bit, and then came up to Miles and licked his hand. "Want some grub? Let's see what they've got in the kitchens for you."

"We can't miss Papa Maracas' spell," said Tom. "Can you hack that, Susan? It would be a shame to miss the ceremony."

"I'll save my collapsing till a bit later," smiled Susan, putting her arms through theirs. "I can't thank you two enough. I thought I was dead."

"Well, you came pretty near to it, I can say," said Miles, grinning from ear to ear with relief.

Back at the school the witch-doctor was drumming his fingers. "Can we please get on?" he said. "For the final time?"

Mr Fox was about to nod, but at the sight of Susan, who had just come through the door, he gave a little hop of relief.

"My dear!" he said, rushing over and shaking her hand and then patting her on the head, the nearest he could get to a kiss. "What you must have been through! Thank goodness you're safe. By the way," he added, "all that nonsense earlier this term, a terrible misunderstanding. Er, ten hundred lettings off for detentions, prize for bravery and all that, OK?"

Susan looked at Tom, who raised his eyebrows. "OK," she said. "As long as you're really sorry."

"I'm really sorry," said Mr Fox. "Really.

Really sorry, very sorry. I'm not just saying it. I'm really…"

Papa Maracas butted in again. "I'm starting this spell now, so please be quiet."

Placing his totems and skulls again in the middle of the room, he then started to dance slowly round the room chanting. He lifted his knees high in the air and Tom and Miles could hardly help laughing, he looked so dotty in Mr Carstairs' flares. After about five minutes, he took a box of matches from his blazer pocket, lit a small cone of incense and threw it up in the air where it exploded into sickly-smelling smoke. Nothing could be seen. Papa Maracas banged his stick on the floor three times.

"Oh, spirit, oh, spirit, who murdered be,
You're trapped and caught and long to be free.
With this strange spell I sign your release
So that you may for ever be at peace!"

At this he clapped his hands and the smoke swirled everywhere. Through it, bright lights and sparks showered out over everyone like fireworks. There were brilliant flashes that lit up Mr Fritz, his brow knotted in concentration, and Mr Fox, shaking his head in a confused kind of way. Then the smoke died down and out of it came a strange white light. Indeed, for one glorious minute the room seemed to be filled with light, dazzling their eyes; then it took off, through the window and out into the open air. Up and up it travelled until it dissolved into the sky. As it did so, the sun burst from behind a cloud and the birds started to sing.

"Happy time!" shouted Papa Maracas. He put his arms round Mr Fox and started to dance with him. Much to everyone's amazement, Mr Fox danced too, and before they knew it they were all gallivanting round the headmaster's study, whooping and crying, until Mrs Grain popped her head round the door and asked what on earth was going on.

"He's gone!" shouted Mr Fritz. "All of them! Lanchester Larry, the poltergeist *and* Ron Grunt!"

"Hurrah!" shouted Mrs Grain, and hurried off to spread the news.

In all the excitement, preparations for Parents' Day were long overdue. During the remainder of the afternoon, work had to be finished off, desks and shoes polished, windows cleaned (they were covered with a kind of sticky green gunge exuded by some weird plant in the South American rain forest), choirs rehearsed, tea arranged, the afternoon's schedule first organized and then photocopied... Mr Fox nearly exploded with anxiety. Much as he loathed Ron Grunt, he could really have done with a caretaker now – or preferably a hundred-strong gang of caretakers who could do all the menial tasks and get the school looking ship-shape. As it was, the pupils had to be roped in to much of the preparations, pupils who should have been learning lines of poetry and rehearsing plays or tidying their rooms.

In order to get things into some kind of order, he allowed the top forms to stay up until half past eleven – but most of them were flagging by ten after their journey into the jungle.

At midnight he slumped into the chair in his office and summoned Mr Fritz.

"Tomorrow – clean the swimming pool; hold final rehearsal of Mozart's *Requiem*; check Form 3's projects and correct spelling mistakes; nail down loose stair-covering, mow back lawn; make sure Asquith Minor has sewn up the hole in his swimming trunks before the diving display; order three hundred dough-nuts from Lanchester to be delivered – plus extra milk; collect extra prospectuses from printers... Mr Fritz, I am exhausted. Is there anything I've left out?"

Mr Fritz cleared his throat. "Only one thing, headmaster. Or, rather, two."

"*Two!*" Mr Fox leaned forward with his eyes bulging. "Don't tell me, Mr Fritz."

"OK," said Mr Fritz, looking anxious. There was a short silence until Mr Fox said, "Well, go on then!"

"Firstly, the witch-doctor. Papa Maracas."

As he spoke these words the science teacher was glad that for once the building didn't shake, nor did a picture fall off the wall. The poltergeist had been well and truly exorcised.

"Hasn't he gone?" groaned Mr Fox.

"I have booked him a flight in the evening. It was the only one I could get. But I'm afraid to say he *will* be around during the day."

At this moment there was a tap on the door. It was Tom.

"Sir," he said, rather nervously.

"Yes?" said Mr Fox crossly. It was high time his pupils were asleep.

"There's an enormous spider in our room. It looks rather like a tarantula. We've dropped a towel over it so it's not moving, but, er, what should we do about it now?"

Mr Fritz clapped a hand to his forehead. "Thank goodness Papa Maracas is here. He'll know what to do."

"OK," said Tom. "I'll go and get him…"

"Just a moment," said Mr Fritz. "You might have some good ideas. The other item, Mr Fox," he said, turning back to the headmaster. "What are you going to say to the parents of the pupils you expelled?"

"Oh, no!" groaned Mr Fox. "As if I didn't have enough on my plate!" He put his head in his hands. "They'll only create the most dreadful trouble. They'll be expecting to take their children home. After having the most ghastly row. No doubt in front of the other parents. I can't bear it!"

They both looked up at Tom expectantly.

"Ask Papa Maracas," he said at once. "He's a witch-doctor. He's bursting with spells. I bet he's got one up his sleeve."

Mr Fox groaned again.

"We've got to wake him up anyway about the spider," said Tom. "I'll ask him."

When the witch-doctor was woken and asked these favours, he sighed. "Everything I will deal with," he said. "But I have just thought – a couple of high-amp speakers I very badly need, plus a fax machine and a small computer I would like. If the headmaster could a few games throw in as well, I'd be glad. I have particularly enjoyed playing this Gameboy of yours. I really don't know why you need to bring me over from the rain forest when such magic of your own you already have."

Tom reassured him that it could all be arranged. "And now, the spider," said Papa Maracas. "Have you a large spade got?"

"Certainly," said Tom, wondering what amazing spells he was going to wreak with a spade. But in the event the witch-doctor simply came to their room, gave the towel a couple of good thumps with the spade, bundled the whole thing up and stuffed it in the waste-paper basket.

"That's how in the jungle we do it," he said.

"Now back to sleep I'm going."

"I will deal with everything" – the phrase the witch-doctor used to reassure Tom about the parents – was not enough to reassure Mr Fox as, from his window, he saw the parents arriving the following afternoon. They rolled up in Bentleys and Range Rovers, Porsches and BMWs. When a strange black car rolled onto the gravel bearing the American flag, Mr Fox felt his stomach turn to knots. Susan's parents. Finding that their daughter wasn't on the flight they expected, they had flown over for an explanation. What was the witch-doctor going to do? And, more important, where was he?

He turned to find Papa Maracas standing behind him, staring over his shoulder. Mr Fox jumped. Then he pointed to Susan's parents.

"That's the girl's parents," he said. "And that – " he added, pointing – "is one of the boys'." Miles' parents had leapt angrily out of their car and were busy conferring with Susan's. They were shaking their heads and occasionally staring up furiously at the headmaster's study window. Mr Fox moved away. "What are you going to do?"

Papa Maracas tapped the bone in his nose. "Have no fear," he said. "Assemble them in your study and introduce me as – as anything you like except myself. A parent, if you like."

"A parent!" said Mr Fox, gaping at his

appearance. "You!"

Papa Maracas looked extremely offended. He cast a black look at Mr Fox. "Your rudeness does not help matters," he said, threateningly. "If I paid you enough money, I am sure you would soon accept me as a parent. But since you are so unwilling to accept my suggestion, then you must introduce me as a new teacher!"

"A new teacher!" Mr Fox's eyes bulged. What kind of teacher would that be, for heaven's sake? He was about to protest but checked himself. He had to go along with Papa Maracas' ideas or all would be lost.

"If you insist," he said rather coldly. He went out to round up the six parents, and ushered them into his study. Everything about them terrified him. They all had lips set like steel traps, and their eyes were blazing. Susan's father carried a sinister long white envelope with a seal on it that looked suspiciously like a writ; Miles' father looked as if he would be quite happy to see the headmaster on the operating table; and Tom's mother, Mrs Buxton, looked like a lioness protecting her cub from an intruder. He was sure that if they were all to look at him simultaneously he would died of hate rays.

"Welcome, welcome!" he croaked, trying to sound cheerful. "Well, we are here to have a discussion! I'm sure everything can be sorted out! Cup of tea? Drink?"

"Drink!" said Mrs Buxton, looking at her watch. "No wonder you can't run this school! It's only half past three!"

"Shocking!" "Preposterous!" "Disgusting!" Burbles of disapproval erupted from everyone's lips like pockets of poison gas from a swamp.

There was a discreet cough from Papa Maracas.

"Ah, before we go any further – may I introduce our newest teacher, Papa Maracas!" said Mr Fox, pushing the witch-doctor forward and praying that things would be all right.

"Teacher!" said Susan's father, staring at him in horror. "Teacher of what?"

"He is our new – er, our new Galanga teacher," said Mr Fox.

"Galanga! What's that?" said Miles' father. "I thought that was a root!"

"No, no," said Mr Fox. "It's a – a language. Forget, er, Japanese. Everyone's speaking Galanga in the business world these days."

"Hajimadeeja, hajimado!" shouted Papa Maracas suddenly, stepping forward dramatically. He held his bony hands high in the air. "Attention please!"

Surprisingly none of the parents moved. Mr Fox stared at them. They seemed mesmerized by the witch-doctor's voice. Then, in a loud ringing tone, he declared:

"None of your children has got to go,
Mr Fox is friend, not foe!
And my final message to you,
Is that you will forget about this spell, too!"

Mr Fox was on tenterhooks. Not only had he threatened to expel all their children, but now he had had them hypnotized by a witch-doctor. He screwed up his eyes and waited. His ears turned purple with anxiety. There was a long silence. He was certain it was going to be broken by threats of writs, threats of violence and, worse, threats of exposure in the Sunday tabloids. Oh, pessimissimus!

Then: "Galanga! I've never heard of that!" Mrs Buxton was looking at him admiringly.

"How original of you, Mr Fox, to organize lessons in this obscure subject! I must find out more. I am sure I will be getting Galangan patients soon. They always drift to Harley Street." Miles' father looked fascinated.

Susan's father clapped him on the back. "I always knew we'd sent Susan to the right school, didn't I, dear," he said to his wife. "Today it's taught at Burlap Hall, tomorrow, the world. I must write a memo about this to the United Nations."

Mr Fox opened his eyes and sighed with relief. The parents' demeanour had completely changed. Papa Maracas was grinning from ear to ear. "To teach the life-style of the Galangans

I am also here to do. To show your English pupils how we live in the Third World. A field trip, you might say."

"Aaah!" "Mmm!" "Fascinating!" and then: "Did I hear you were going to perform Mozart's *Requiem*?" and "Did you mention tea?" And with that the parents shuffled from the room, beaming.

Mr Fox took out his handkerchief and mopped his brow. He held out his hand. "I can't thank you enough, Papa Maracas," he said. He even considered asking if he'd care to be bought a pint at the local. "I shall call Tom and ask him to accompany you to the shops. Please – let me give you a blank cheque up to say – what – ten pounds? I hope this will cover your needs."

He hurried off to greet a bunch of new parents who were assembled on the lawn, waiting for a tour of the school. "Forgive me. A little business," he said. "And now I expect you'll want to inspect the new science block before we witness the diving display. Do follow me."

Parents' Day finally ended. By six o'clock the gravel on the drive had been well and truly crunched in as the cars set off for their various destinations. On the whole it had been a success, thought Mr Fox as he sat, exhausted, with his feet up in his study, having a glass of whisky. Twenty new parents had signed their children up for the following year. Things weren't too bad after all. Then he heard the revving up of a final car. Getting to his feet, he looked out of the window. Below, Tom, Miles and Susan were loading boxes of electrical equipment into Mr Fritz's battered old Morris van. Mr Fox wondered what on earth it all was. It must have cost a fortune! They must have added at least two noughts to that cheque for ten pounds he'd given them. Oh, well, it was worth it, he supposed. Papa Maracas, still in his maroon-and-yellow-striped blazer (Mr Carstairs hadn't liked to ask for it back) was rubbing his hands as he watched. Mr Fritz was in the driving seat, warming up the engine. Finally they all got in and Mr Fritz moved slowly away. Off to the airport, thought Mr Fox. Peace at last. But as he relaxed into his chair he suddenly heard the car stopping in the drive. He got up and stared out of the window again. Surely there wasn't a last minute hold-up?

"Sir, sir!" Tom had got out of the car and was waving at him and pointing. There, hobbling down the drive, was a familiar figure. Bent almost double and tottering on a couple of crutches was none other than Mr Crumbly, the old caretaker.

"Hello, Miss Susan, Mr Miles, Mr Tom – and, sir!" he chirped, waving at everyone in the car. Then he looked up and saw Mr Fox. "I'm

back at last, sir! So – how have you been getting on without me?"

Tom gave a grin and waved at Mr Fox as he
got back into the car. And, revving up the
engine, Mr Fritz drove off in the direction of
the airport.

Mr Fox hurried downstairs to greet the
caretaker.

"My dear man! Is it really you? I hope my
minces don't deceive me!" he said, putting his
arm round him and hugging him like an old
friend. "We had quite given you up! We have
been through the most *terrible* time without
you! Now come up and join me in a drink."

And together they made their way up the
apples and pears, laughing and joking, to Mr
Fox's study.